MW01490124

Every great dream begins with a dreamer.
Always remember, you have within you the
strength, the patience, and the passion to reach
for the stars to change the world.

                    Harriet Tubman

It had been a long week at Russell, McKay and Dublin Property Investments, one of the largest African American owned investment companies in Atlanta, Georgia. As Rachel Abney was getting ready to shut it down for a weekend of well deserved rest, she could not help but regale in her latest acquisition of a $305 million dollar property that will triple in value and continue to bring in a continuous income once developed. It has been a long journey for Rachel as she worked her way up from entry level Loan Officer to the head of the company's Property Acquisition's department, but it was well worth the trip. She oversees one hundred-fifty employees. Her secretary Sarah buzzed,

"Ms. Abney, Mr. McKay is on line one for you." Rachel picked up the receiver.

"Yes Mr. McKay what can I do for you?" Rachel asked with a broad grin on her face.

"Rachel, you and your team were great. It took six months, but you managed to acquire the most sought after property that four other companies have been trying to obtain for two years. My hat goes off to you and your team. Not only will you receive your bonus, but your team will receive a hefty bonus, and an all expenses paid trip to Hawaii. Please inform them that their families will be invited also. Again, congratulations. Now get out of the office and enjoy your weekend. We will start training for another sparring match on Monday."

"Thank you Mr. McKay. I will inform my team of your generous gift. On behalf of my team, it was tough but it was our pleasure. You also have a good weekend and I will see you on Monday" was Rachel's response.

Rachel sat down in her high back chair and swiveled around to look out over the city and just smiled. She was thinking about what had just happened and how she had gotten to this point. The hard work, sweat and sacrifices had finally paid off. A light knock on her office door interrupted her thoughts.

"Ms. Abney, will there be anything else?" her secretary inquired.

"No Sarah. You go home and have a great weekend. Also, thank you for all of your help. The last couple of weeks I have kept you late and I could not have done it without you keeping me organized and on track. Take

Monday off and I will see you first thing on Tuesday."

"Thank you Ms. Abney. You have a good weekend also."

"Goodnight."

With that Sarah stepped back out and closed the door behind her. Rachel started gathering her things but hesitated and sat back down. She returned to looking out of the window. As good as she felt at that moment, she could not help but feel a little melancholy. She was happy about the current events of the company, but there was no one outside of the office to share them with. While working hard striving to be the best, there was no time for a personal life. She had plenty of dinner dates but felt the time was not right to get distracted from her rise to the top in the company. When she had decided to relax a little and go with the flow, after three years, it turned out to be a disastrous relationship and she decided not to entangle herself ever again. She hurt so much after that relationship she decided never again. Besides, she had things to do and goals to reach. With that last thought she swiveled her chair back around. She took off her heels and slid into her loafers and prepared to leave.

Rachel gathered the last of her things and headed out the door. As she awaited the elevator she was thinking about the relaxing weekend she was going to enjoy. She was going to try not to think about work if at all possible. When the elevator arrived Kyle the elevator man greeted her.

"Good evening Ms. Abney. Heading home for the weekend?" he inquired.

"Hello Kyle. Yes I am. It has been a long, but profitable week" was her reply.

When they reached the ground floor they said their good-byes and she headed toward the garage to retrieve her car. Kyle continued to follow Rachel with his eyes until she was out of sight. Every since he laid eyes on her he somehow knew this was the woman he has been praying for. The only problem is that after four years in the company as the elevator man he could not get up the nerve to ask her out. Besides he thought, she is out of his league. The elevator doors closed and he went back to work.

Meanwhile, Rachel was piling into her 2011 fully loaded, metallic blue Jaguar. The car was a beauty. She paid three fourths of the total amount in cash with the rest in monthly payments. By her estimation the car will be paid in full in about two years. Instead of rushing out into the afternoon traffic she just sat for a minute. Once she decided to get going, she looked for some driving music to put in her CD player. Rachel was trying to decide what type of mood she was in for the drive home. She opted for smooth jazz. She started the car and eased into the traffic for the 45 minute drive home.

As the music played Rachel was going back over the events of the week that led up to the acquisition. A smile arose on her face and she relaxed and tapped her fingers to the music of Kenny G. Once she reached the highway leading out of the city, she made a right on Ravenswood highway and headed toward home. The drive was uneventful and quiet. It was only

4:30 p.m. and the sun was still high in the sky. There were clouds scattered sparsely throughout the sky but no threat of rain.

Rachel finally reached the gated community where she lived. This community, Havenhurst Village, was a quaint little town all by itself. It consisted of a Grocery store, hardware store, pet store, post office, bank, a bistro and of course a Burger King, which was her favorite, and other great amenities. When she pulled up in front of her place of residence the doorman, Ralph, opened the door for her and the valet proceeded to park her car. She lived in a twenty story high rise condominium. Once she entered the elevator Maurice greeted her.

"Good evening Ms. Abney. How are you this fine day?" Maurice asked.

"Hello Maurice. I am doing just fine. I am looking forward to a much needed weekend without the thought of work." Rachael said.

When they reached the top floor, the doors open, she got off and headed toward her condo which was two doors from the elevator. She opened her door, stepped inside, took a deep breath and said to herself, "home at last." Rachel began to feel the events of the day and the entire week slowly closing behind her as the door closed. She took her shoes off and stepped down into the living room of her condo onto the soft, thick white carpet. She sighed with pleasure as she began to walk toward her bedroom, shedding clothing as she walked. The thought of a relaxing weekend after a long week of wheeling and dealing with negotiations and finally closing the deal was making Rachel elated with excitement. By the time she reached her bedroom all she had on was her underclothes. She threw her clothes on the bed, grabbed her robe and sat on her bed to think for a minute.

Rachel had just moved into her new condo when the negotiations were getting started. Because of the demands of her job she had to pay an interior decorator to do what she wanted. She gave the information to the decorators and they went about their work. Rachel looked around and admired what they had done. It was actually the way she had envisioned the place to be. Actually, she thought, this will be the first time she will actually be able to enjoy her home.

Rachel's bedroom was large and luxurious. Covering her queen size bed was a down feather bedspread. The design was one of a large lion on the top with a Safari background. The pillow cases and shams were a perfect match. The color scheme for the room was earth tones with designs of an African motif. There were African artifacts scattered throughout the room. It was on her vacation to South Africa that gave her the decorating ideas. She figured this would be her way of reliving a wonderful time in her life. The different masks that hug on the wall were authentic and shipped directly from Africa.

On her vanity were the usual female products such as her perfumes, makeup and jewelry. Her mirror, which was oval shaped, had carvings of flowers and leaves etched into the wood finish. Surrounding the mirror were pictures of her family. The pictures were of her mother and father, her grandparents, and

siblings, a brother and sister. Rachel also had

pictures of her four nieces and two nephews.

There was a small, brown statue of a woman

cradling her newborn looking down upon her

child with love. She received the statue from a

friend about six years ago. It was given to her

at a time in her life when, what was to be a

wonderful event, turned into a nightmare. There

is a night stand on each side of her bed. On the

side in which she generally sleeps, she has a

lamp shaped in the form of a panther, with the

base formed like paws. The mouth of the

panther is opened where the light bulb is placed.

The shade covering the lamp was

tan with desert background. There were bushes

and an occasional tree with an oasis and a

watering hole. The panther was chasing its

prey. Rachel is a voracious reader, sometimes reading three books at a time. She is currently reading "The Audacity of Hope" by Barack Obama, "The Heart of a Woman" by Maya Angelou, and "The Other Woman" by Eric Jerome Dickey. Her taste in reading material is vast and goes from one end of the spectrum to the other.

The other night stand has the same lamp, but the reading material on this side of the bed contains materials from work. She would often bring work home in order to stay ahead of the game. She has worked too hard to get to where she is. Rachel has her sights on a higher mountain peak and will not let anything or anyone get in her way. With her relaxation minute over she decides to take a hot soothing soak in her tub that doubles as a Jacuzzi. Once she starts the water running, Rachel goes to the kitchen and pours herself a glass of wine. After taking a sip, she grabs the bottle and heads back to the bathroom. She turns off the water and prepares to embark on a long sensuous soak to erase away the tensions of not only that day but the months leading up to this point. Rachel's love of music is as vast as her reading material. She proceeds to turn on the CD player that is mounted on the wall of the bathroom. John Legend was slow grooving on his piano while singing a love ballad.

Rachel stands about 5 feet 10 inches tall. Her complexion is caramel with brown eyes and golden bronze hair that hangs down just below her shoulders. She has perfect white pearl teeth with a smile that lights up any room, when she relaxes enough to do so. As she steps out of her robe she swishes the water to ensure the bubbles were evenly distributed throughout. Rachel steps into the tub and, once she is settled she takes another sip of her wine, leans her head back and exhales slowly. She smiled as she started thinking about the weekend ahead.

While basking in the warmth of the sudsy Jacuzzi with the jet spray on low, Rachel drifted off to sleep. Not realizing just how tired she really was, a deep sleep overtook her and she began to dream. This dream took her back several years. It was about seven years ago that she met Robert Louis Jones, Esq. He was a partner in the very prestigious law firm of Morris, Conrad and Jones that specialize in corporate law. Though both of their schedules were hectic at the time, they made sure to set aside time to date and were getting quite close.

Things were starting to heat up and after dating for two years, they began talking about marriage. Into the third year of the relationship Rachel became pregnant. Though they were busy trying to schedule a wedding the news was welcomed with excitement. This pushed the timing of the wedding to take place before the baby was born. In her mind everything was fine. What Rachel did not know was that Robert, her husband to be and the father of their unborn child was turning into somebody she did not recognize. This was not the same man she had met three years prior.

The signs had been there all along, though very subtle. There were the mood swings, and the snapping at her for no apparent reason. They started going out together less and less and he was working late more and more.

Rachel pushed it aside and thought it was just the pressures of work and paid it no mind. Then one day while cooking dinner for the two of them he came home, went to the bedroom and slammed the door shut. She turned the eyes of the stove off and went to find out what was going on. When she opened the door, to her horror she saw him put something up his nose.

"Robert, what are doing? What was that you just sniffed up your nose?"

"Don't start with the questions. I have had a hard day. What's for dinner?"

"Not until you tell me what you are doing.

Robert had lifted his head from his hands and looked at her with disgust. Then like a tiger after stalking its prey, he quickly jumped to his feet and had her by the shoulders and pushing her against the wall.

"Robert", she screamed, "you are hurting me."

"I'm going to do more than that if you don't leave me the hell alone and get my dinner."

With that he shoved her out of the bedroom. Rachel stumbled out of the room careful not to fall because of the three month baby she was carrying. Crying, she went to the kitchen to finish dinner but was dumbfounded as to what was happening. When she finished she went to the bedroom to let him know that it was ready, and as she approached the room she overheard him on the telephone. Instead of going in she decided to see if she could get some insight and began to listen.

"Listen baby, I will be over as soon as I can. She does not suspect a thing. What? No I did not tell her about my job, why? Look, you handle things the way you have been and I will take care of things over here. I got to go. I will be there when she falls asleep. Yeah, I love you too. Peace."

With her mouth covered in astonishment, she backed away from the door. She went into the bathroom, turned on the faucet and just looked into the mirror. There were tears running down her face like the water that was coming from the faucet. Rachel heard a bang on the door that startled her.

"What are you doing in there? Is dinner ready?"

"Coming," she said as calmly as she could.

She cupped her hands and put some cold water on her face. After that she wiped her face with the washcloth, checked herself in the mirror and opened the door. Robert was standing there with this hardened look on his face.

"What took you so long?"

"I was feeling sick. You scared me and shoved me kind of hard."

"Whatever. Is my dinner ready?"

"Yes."

She just looked at him and could not figure out what to do or say about what she had just heard so she decided to just wait.

"Well, what are you waiting on? Let's eat."

They went into the dining room and as he sat down, she went to get their plates. There was so much tension in the air it was like being in a really darkened room trying to feel your way to the light switch.

"So, how was your day?"

"What's that suppose to mean?" Robert said while lifting food to his mouth and glaring at her.

"Nothing in particular, accept you when came home from work you went straight to the bedroom. When I come to see what is wrong, you are shoving stuff up your nose and then when I ask you about it you jump on me like I just accused of killing someone. Is there something you want to tell me? "

"Look, I just had a hard day. And as far as the other stuff is concerned, you are not naïve. It just takes the edge off. I have it under control and I am not a drug addict or anything. Besides, what business is it of yours anyway?"

"It is my business because we are going to be married and I am carrying your child. I have a right to know what I am getting myself into. And by the way, what about your job don't I know about? And who are you saying 'I love you' to besides me?"

Robert stood up cleared the table in one sweep and leaped toward her. She tried to get up but did not move fast enough.

"Where are you going?"

"I was just trying to go to the kitchen. Robert, what are you doing? No, don't do that. Think about the baby."

"This baby is all I've been hearing about for the last three months and it is actually getting on my nerves. If you lose this baby I will be okay. What about you?"

While talking to her, he started slapping her in the face and as she was wailing in fear she took the hits and covered her belly with her hands and arms hoping to keep the blows there. It didn't work. When he saw what she was doing, he grabbed her by the hair and swung her around then let go of her in mid flight. Landing with a thud, she coward in a fetal position and did not move. His rage and anger getting more intense, Robert was breathing like a bull in a search of its next breath. He walked over to Rachel in a deliberate march to check to see if she was still alive. The closer he got to her the more he could hear her whimpering. As if the damage he had done to her was not enough, he lifted her like a rag doll and threw her stomach first into the wall. It was after this last violent act that Rachel passed out.

Because of the commotion, an elderly neighbor that Rachel had befriended decided to check on her. As she was about to ring the doorbell, Robert had his coat in hand and was coming out of the door.

"Is everything ok?" Mrs. Campbell asked.

"Who wants to know?" he asked with a growl and a huff.

"I'm your next door neighbor and I was taking a nap and was awakened by loud thud against the wall in my bedroom."

"Everything is fine. I was hanging a picture and bumped the wall trying to catch balance after almost falling."

"Oh. I was just concerned that your wife may have injured herself. That would not be good in the precious condition she is in. Is she in? She is a sweet girl. She takes time to talk to me all the time. I get lonely because my family is scattered about. So when is......."

"Look, I will tell her you stopped by. I am in a hurry for an appointment."

"I'm sorry. I do tend to just rattle on. Well tell her I will stop back later."

With that Robert stepped back inside to give the lady time to go inside of her apartment. Once he was confident she was in he left and locked the door behind him, leaving Rachel on the floor bleeding profusely. Little did he know was that Rachel and Mrs. Campbell were closer than he thought. Because of his working all the time, they exchanged keys in case of an emergency. Mrs. Campbell was looking out of her peephole to ensure that he had left and decided to knock on the door to check. As she was putting the key in the lock she called out to Rachel.

"Rachel, it's me, Mrs. Campbell. Are you here?

There was no answer. What she noticed walking in was the mess in the apartment. With trepidation she walked through the living room and just as she was about to turn and walk into the dining room, she saw Rachel lying on the floor. With a grief stricken look she bent down to see if she was breathing.

"Oh my God, Rachel, what happened?" Unsure if she heard her, she decided to softly rub the palm of her hand against her cheek. She began to stir slightly.

"Rachel, I am going to call an ambulance and the police. You are going to be alright."

Rachel looked up at Mrs. Campbell, but her eyes were closed shut and she could not see her clearly. She tried to speak but nothing came out. After slightly clearing her throat, all she could do was cover her stomach tighter, but she could only begin to cry again. After calling the police Mrs. Campbell found a washcloth, wet it with cold water and went to be by her side. While talking to her, she began wiping her face as gingerly as she could.

"I saw your fiancé. He said you were ok. When he left I decided to come and check on you. Did he do this to you, honey?"
In response, the only thing she could do was nod her head in the affirmative. Just then there was a knock on the door. Mrs. Campbell let in the police and the ambulance workers were coming down the hall behind them. She

explained what she knew of the situation, including the conversation with the fiancé.

She spent three weeks in the hospital. The doctors did all they could to save the baby but there was too much damage. Robert came by only at night for fear of the police. He was very sorry and was begging her not leave him.

. "I promise I will get help. Just don't leave me" he said. Rachel started to stir in her sleep as the painful events unfolded once again.

Some time had passed and things were starting to get back to normal, whatever normal was after something as traumatic as the events of the last month. Robert did not or would not explain why he started using drugs. For that matter he did not apologize for anything. Rachel found out later that he was embezzling money to support his drug habit. The partners wanted to buy him out before it became public but Robert was arrogant about the situation and would not sell his share of the business. The partners had no choice but to file criminal charges on him and let the courts handle it. On top of everything else, she found out that he had been seeing an old girlfriend from almost the entire time they were together. Once Rachel confronted him about the information she had, he finally decided to tell the truth.

"Rachel, I proposed marriage only because I did not want you to find out what I was really up to. You were making all the wedding plans and spending your money. I figured I would go along and not show up at the ceremony. No loss to me or my money."

Her face had the look as though someone just punched her in the stomach.

"And by the way, I AM getting married to my girlfriend who I have been seeing that last two years. You were just a distraction while we worked out our difficulties."

Robert was very smug as he put in the knife and turned. Rachel started to cry. As the dream progressed forward, Rachel began to stir once more. She started thinking about her parents and how close they had been at one time. Things began to change when she decided to be with Robert in spite of their strong opposition. There was some things said that she regrets every day. Though she knows they were ultimately right, and that they love her, it is hard for her to swallow her pride and call them. It has been two years since she last spoke to her parents. She talks to her brother and sister often along with her nieces and nephews. They urge her to call their parents but it is hard. Tears start to fall down her cheeks and she begins to awaken.

Rachel shakes herself and begins to wash. She is clearly shaken but lets the emotion of sadness roll off her back like the water while rinsing off. Once she has completed her bath, Rachel realizes she has not eaten since early this afternoon. The growl in her stomach was singing the song of hunger. She leaves her bedroom and heads toward the kitchen. On her way she goes to the balcony to open the doors to let the warm night air breeze its way through the spacious penthouse. As she walks towards the kitchen she pauses to check the blinking light on the answering machine. There were three calls.

One was from another partner in the firm congratulating her and her team on the acquisition. The second was from her sister checking on her and the last call was from her best friend Allana Forest. She was in town and wanted to get together.

She and Allana grew up together in Fort Lauderdale, Florida and had a bond like no other. They had been there for each others ups and downs. They went to Spellman College together, graduated and pursued their passions in different states. Through all of this they managed to stay connected as friends, comrades and home girls. Allana was married and had a son, who should be about seventeen. Rachel was excited and decided that she would call her when she was finished eating.

Rachel decided to eat on the balcony overlooking the area in which she lived. The lights were beginning to brighten the streets below her. The sun in the horizon gave a beautiful array of colors of orange and yellow as it began to settle down for the night. Rachel sat down to prepare to partake in a delicious meal of baked pork chops seasoned to taste, a baked sweet potato, steamed vegetables and a side salad. Of course there was the glass of wine. As she began to eat she started thinking about the dream. She had long put those events behind her. They were too painful to think about, especially the loss of her child.

After that tumultuous time in her life, along with the loss of contact with her parents, she threw herself into her work. Dating was out of the question. She went out on occasion but nothing serious. She vowed she would never give her heart to another. As she ate the last bite of her pork chop and finished her cup of wine, she thought how delightful and filling her dinner had been. Rachel stood up from the table took a deep breath and went to the kitchen to clean the dishes. Once that was completed she decided to call Allana. She heads back to the balcony and situates herself on the chaise lounge. She dials the number and it rang twice before she heard the voice of her friend.

"Hey girl" Rachel said.

"Rachel? I am so glad you could tear yourself away from work to call me. How are you doing?

"Whatever girl, you know I'll call you if I don't call anyone else. I'm just fine. What brings you to the ATL?"

"Well Rachel, I have some news for you. Are you going to be busy this weekend? I will be in town until Tuesday. Can we get together?"

"Actually Allana, you could not have come at a more perfect time. I just finished this deal and I will be doing ALAP. That is as little as possible", she said with a giggle. "Is everything ok?" Rachel asked with a little concern in her voice.

"We will talk about it when I see you" was Allana's response.

"Tell you what", Rachel said. "Let's get together tomorrow for lunch. I'm going to work out, run some errands and I will meet you at Café Romero's at 1:00pm. Is that soon enough for you?"

Allana hesitated and then said,

"That will be great. I'll see you then. In the mean time have a good evening. I am so glad to talk to you. It has been too long."

"I will see you tomorrow."

Rachel hung up the phone and stared out over the horizon in thought. I wonder what is going on with her she thought. She felt worry starting to creep in and she shook it off and decided to wait until they talked before coming to any conclusion that may or may not be true. Once that thought was taken care of she decided to go in and read a little. She went to the bedroom, prepared her bed and crawled under the cover. Rachel picked up her book and read a few lines. She closed the book and decided she was too tired to concentrate. As she slid down in the bed she did not realize how tired she was and drifted immediately to sleep.

The next day, after years of conditioning, Rachel awakened, looked at the clock only for it to read 6 a.m. She fell back in the bed and groaned. Just once, she thought, I would like to sleep at least until 8:00am. After lying there for a few more minutes she got up and went to the kitchen to start a pot of hot water for tea. While the water was getting hot she took a quick shower, put on her workout clothes and tennis shoes. By the time she finished the tea kettle was whistling. She made her some toast with butter and honey. Rachel was excited about seeing her buddy later that day. Once the tea and toast were consumed she snatched up her keys and ID and went to the exercise room in the building.

As usual, Maurice was on his post. When the door opened he greeted Rachel with a broad grin on his face.

"Good Morning. How are you doing this fine day? You are up pretty early for a Saturday." Maurice said to Rachel.

Rachel smiled.

"Good morning. I am doing well, and you?"

Maurice was caught off guard. She usually just smiled and continued her private thoughts. He thought maybe this was his chance to start a conversation.

"Actually, I am doing great. God has blessed me to see another day" was Maurice response.

Rachel looked at him with a look of disbelief. She knows there is a God. Her parents took her to church when she was a child, but since she became an adult she felt no need to go to church or have anything to do with God. To keep from being rude, her only response was, "that's nice."

By this time the elevator had reached it's destination of the exercise room. The doors opened and Maurice, with a grin on his face said,

"Have a blessed workout." With that the doors closed before Rachel had chance to respond.

She went into the room and saw that she was not alone, even this early in the morning. Rachel started to stretch for a few minutes. Once the stretching was complete she headed toward the stationary bikes. After situating herself on the bike she started her peddling. The television was on the CNN channel and she decided to get caught up on the world events since she did not watch much television at home.

As the riding became more intense Rachel started scanning the room. She noticed a lot of people she had never seen before. While looking around, her eyes stopped in the area of the barbells. She could not believe what she saw. Her disbelief was such that she had to do a double take. Her eyes gazed upon the most wonderful looking hard body. Rachel stopped peddling when she saw that the beautiful body belonged to James Rivers. This guy was someone who she had not seen in at least twenty years. He was actually her first love.

Rachel had begun to think about the last time she saw James. It was their high school graduation. They had been together since eighth grade and they were to be together forever. After the graduation party he dropped the bomb. He had joined the military and would be leaving in two days. He asked her to wait on him but she was not sure. They were going to go to college together, graduate, start their careers and get married. Now he wants her to wait on him. She couldn't do it. As much as she loved him she knew that a long distant relationship was not going to work.

The day he left she decided that they should just go their separate ways. The decision was a hard one to make but she had to free him and herself to pursue their lives without conflict or hang-ups. As she was admiring his look a slight grin came across her face when she noticed there was no ring on his finger. When she caught herself in a stare she quickly went back to her peddling on her stationary bike. As she began to get back into her rhythm she started rationalizing how she did not have time to be involved in any relationship right now. Before she could divert her mind to something more practical, like the television, there was a tap on her shoulder. When she turned around she noticed a beautiful smile on the face of an old friend.

"Hey there beautiful, how have you been?" James asked.

"James, it's been a long time. How long have you been standing there?" Rachel asked.

"Long enough, I caught you looking at me and I just wanted to come over to let you know." He said smiling.

"I was not." Rachel said with a broad grin.

With that they both broke into laughter. Rachel got off of the stationary bike and they embraced. All Rachel could think of was how she had forgotten how good she felt in his arms. He still smells good too, even after a workout. They began to separate but James did not let go. He just stared into her eyes.

"Rachel, your eyes are still as beautiful as I remember."

"Thank you" was all she could muster up to say while pulling from him. Reluctantly he let her go.

"So tell me Rachel, what have you been up to these days? I hear you're a big time property mogul now." he said with a grin.

"Actually" she began with a smug look on her face, but smiling broadly, "I am the head of the Property Acquisitions' department in my company. I would not say that I am a mogul but I do alright for myself. How did you hear about me anyway?"

"I asked around. I stopped by to see your parents before I came to Atlanta. They told me that even though they hadn't spoken to you for a while that you were doing great and they were proud of your accomplishments." The smile left Rachel's face and she leaned against the treadmill and folded her arms. The mention of her parents was a touchy subject right now since she has not spoken to them in quite a while. When James noticed the change in her attitude he inquired as to what was the problem.

"Did I say something wrong?" James asked.

Rachel just gave him that look that she used to so many years ago. "No. It's just that I have not spoken to my parents in a while and for some reason it touched a nerve."

"And why is that?" James pressed. Rachel let out a loud sigh and said,

"I really don't want to get into it right now. So, how long are you going to be here in Atlanta?" Rachel asked changing the subject. James looked at her and instead of pushing the issue he figured he would do better to leave well enough alone.

"Well, I am not for sure. I am here for a Minister's Conference and for the most part it ends on Friday of next week." James answered.

"What kind of conference? Please don't tell me you bootlegging as a preacher," she said with a chuckle. Rachel took a step backwards and just looked at him.

"First of all, I'm not bootlegging. Second, since the last time you saw me there have been some changes in my life that will take some time to explain. I tell you what, why don't we get together for dinner tonight and we can talk then. How about seven o'clock."

"I have a lunch appointment at one o'clock. Where are you staying?"

"I'm staying with some friends here in the building. What floor are you on and I'll pick you up." James asked.

Taken aback, Rachel decided to take precautionary steps.

"Tell you what, why don't we just meet in the lobby and we can go from there."

James grinned and said "That will be fine. I'll see you at seven o'clock."

With that James turned and headed toward the showers. Rachel on the other hand decided to workout a little longer. She found her way to the treadmill, put the settings in place and got on. As she started her walk her mind began to go back to what just transpired. Rachel was thinking about the impending dinner and the conversation that she and James just had. She thought how James was still good looking, with loads of charm. Only now he seems to be a bit reserved.

He was always a character, always telling jokes and having a good time while striving for the best. He was valedictorian of our class, left to go to the military and to pursue his dreams. Yet he seems different. There is something about him that is not the same as he was when we were dating and going to school. Of course everyone grows up but, this is something different.

Rachel finished her time on the treadmill. Once she checked her watch she decided to go run some errands and then prepare herself for her lunch date with her best girlfriend, whom she has not seen in a while. Her friend Allana sounded like something was going on.

They decided to meet at an Italian Bistro right in the heart of downtown. Once she found a parking space she locked her car and started to walk the half block. As she approached the restaurant she could see her friend sitting at one of the tables on the outside. Allana was looking at a menu and did not see her friend walk up.

"Hey girl, is there anything good on that menu?" Rachel said as she stood in the light of the sun.

"Nope, but I'm hungry so I'll find something to eat" as Allana looked up to see her friend standing there.

They laughed and hugged each other then she sat down.

"Rachel, how are you doing? It has been a long time. What's been going on with you?" Allana asked with excitement.

"Well, I've been just trying to maintain the status quo. You know, stay strong, stay black, and make all the money I can." Rachel answered with a chuckle.

"I understand that. Have you talked to your parents lately?"

"Not in about two years. Why?" the tone changing in her voice.

"Girl, calm down. I was just asking. Anyway, what do you do for entertainment? Is there a special someone I should know about?" Allana asked with a Cheshire cat-like grin on her face.

Rachel changed her demeanor and returned to smiling.

"Allana, I am too busy to have a real social life. After that last disaster, well you know I am not feeling that or anyone right now. Mind you, I have friends. An occasional dinner date but that is as far as it goes. Besides, I do have to eat you know" she said smiling.

The waiter came to their table.

"Hello. My name is Michael and I will be your server today. May I get you ladies something to drink?"

"I'll have a raspberry tea with lemon" Allana said.

"I'll have a top shelf long island iced tea." Rachel said.

"Can I get you an appetizer?" the waiter asked.

"None for me thank you, how about you Allana?"

"No thank you" was her reply.

"Very well, I will return with your drinks momentarily."

"Thank you" they said in unison. As they browsed the menu for something to eat, Rachel began talking.

"So Allana, what have you been up to? I haven't heard from you in a while."

"A lot has been going on. For one thing, I went back to school to get my Bachelor's Degree in Business with a minor in Accounting. I just finished and will be graduating in January."

"Congratulations girl. I had no idea you were going. Why didn't you tell me?"

"I have been saying that I was going back for at least three years. Every time I said it out loud, something would come up and get in the way. So I decided to not talk about it but be about it. Savione' has been great. He helped out with Davione' and the household stuff, cooking and cleaning, just so I can study and do my thing. We have been married for fifteen years and instead of us settling into a rut, we are learning more about each other, which has helped us to love and appreciate each other more."

"Girl, you have always been the sentimental type. Just wait until you hit the twenty year mark. You will be singing a new song."

"Come on Rachel, why you hatin' on a sista?" Allana asked as she began to laugh.

"I'm not hatin' on you. Actually I am happy for you. I'm glad someone can find happiness with that special someone. You know where I've been and it is not happening." Rachel said with a smug look on her face. "Never say never because you don't know who God has for you."

Rachel was taken aback by that last comment of her friend. She just looked at her and realized that she was the second, no make that the third person today who has said something about or in reference to God. She is starting to get suspicious of her friend and just came out and asked her.

"Okay Allana, what's really going on?" Allana continued to look at the menu.

"What? What are you talking about?"

"Well, first you show up in Atlanta without calling, and now you are talking about what God may have for me. Did my mother send you here?" Rachel replied.
Just as Allana was putting her menu aside, the waiter showed up with their drinks.

"Here are your drinks ladies." Michael stated. Once he placed their drinks down he asked, "Are you ready to order?"

"I'll have the Fettuccine Alfredo with chicken. May I have extra sauce please?"

"Sure. No problem. What can I get for you ma'am?" Michael said looking at Rachel.

"I'll have the spaghetti and meatballs with extra sauce." Rachel added.

"I'll be back with your orders as soon as they are ready. Can I get you anything else?" They both nodded their head no and the waiter turned and went to another table.

Allana took a sip of her drink and Rachel did the same. When they put their drinks down Rachel began speaking again.

"Now back to the question I had asked you."

"What question is that?" Allana asked. In her mind she was praying and asking God to help her explain what was going on and that her friend would be receptive to the good news.

"Don't play with me Allana. You know exactly what question I'm talking about. But just in case you have amnesia, what is going on?" Rachel said in a more serious but bordering on agitated tone this time.

Allana looked at her friend. She could see that Rachel was in pain but hiding it well from those who did not know her. Prayerfully the news of her growing relationship with God will help her. Maybe she will see that she can hide from everybody but the one who knows her best because He created her.

"Well Rachel, something has been going on. It is not a bad thing. Actually it is quite good." Allana began.

"Allana, are you pregnant again?" Rachel asked.

"No. Well I don't think so." Allana answered giggling.

"Well, spit it out. What is it?"

"Rachel, I hope you understand but if not I will be more than willing to explain."

"Allana if you don't tell me what is going on I am going strangle you. Now what is it?"

"The most wonderful thing happened to me. Let me see, it was a Tuesday night. I was visiting this church, The Church of Truth. The pastor was talking about being born again."

"Aw, come on Allana. You didn't, did you?"

"Didn't do what? What he was talking about was very interesting. You know how we used to go to church when we were younger but we could care less. We just went because our parents made us. And when we were there, we sat with our friends and talked through the whole service. Laughing and playing and not paying attention."

"Yeah, I never could or wanted to hear what was being said. The singing was good but once the preacher started talking I zoned out in my own head if I was not clowning around."

"Well, after high school graduation I stopped going to church because I felt that it was not for me. Mom and Dad could not force me to go anymore so I stopped. We went to college, graduated and pursued our goals in separate states, but something was missing in my life." Allana said.

As she picked up her glass to take a sip, Rachel was studying her friend and could not believe what she was hearing.

"I know we have talked in this last year. So why haven't you told me this. Why come all the way to Atlanta. This is something you could have told me over the telephone." Rachel said feeling herself getting upset.

"Why are you getting angry?"

"Because I thought we were friends. I thought we tell each other everything. I don't know who you are anymore." Rachel said with a look of a person who just lost her best friend.

"Rachel, I wanted to tell you but I needed to learn about this stuff myself. The pastor was talking about how no matter how successful you are in this life that it means nothing to God if He is not a part of it. God has given us the talents and skills and blessings to do what we do but not knowing Him in a real and personal way and living for Him is a sure way of being left behind. I know this is a lot for you to take in right now. Once I started studying I wanted to share the good news with you. When I realized I was coming to Atlanta for business I thought this would be a good time."

Rachel was sitting and staring at her friend who she thought she knew. She picked up her drink, took a gulp and called for their waiter to ask for another drink.

"Allana, after everything we have been through you could not have given me a heads up about this? You could have said something in our telephone conversations. I had no clue."

"Rachel why are you so angry? It's not like I killed somebody. I thought this was going to be good news."

"Girl, at this moment I don't know what to think or why I am angry. Look, here comes our food. Let's eat and try to get back to enjoying each other's company and the food okay?" Rachel said while she pasted a half hearted smile on her face.

The food was excellent. They ate in almost total silence before Rachel spoke up and said. "Allana, we have been friends since grade school. I do not begrudge you a better spiritual life. If this is what you need then you do what you do. Just don't start preaching to me because I have gotten along just fine to this point without "God" and I will continue to do so. Besides serving a God that may or may not be real is not for everybody. Everybody is spiritual in their own way.

"Girl, I am not going to preach to you. I will be and have been praying for you. I love you and don't want anything but for you to experience the full and complete joy of having a relationship with someone who will not only love you unconditionally, but who gave his life for you."

"You sound like the Sunday School teachers we heard when we were young and dumb." Rachel said with a laugh.

"Hold on now" Allana said, "We were young but I refuse to say I was dumb. You were maybe, but definitely not me." Rachel continued while snickering.

They both broke out in laughter. The tension appeared to have been broken slightly. Rachel decided to change the subject.

"You will never guess who I ran into while working out this morning."

"I can't imagine." Allana said.

Just as Rachel was about to tell her, Michael, the waiter came over.

"Would you ladies like some dessert this afternoon?"

"As tempting as that sounds, I better not. What about you Allana?"

"If I do then I will be in the gym the rest of my stay. I'll pass." Allana told the waiter chuckling.

"As I said, I ran into an old friend this morning. Do you remember James Rivers?" Rachel asked taking a sip of her drink.

Allana's eyes began to widen then a broad smile crept upon her face.

"Of course I remember James. You two were inseparable. Where did you say you ran into him?" Allana asked.

"I saw him while I was working out this morning. He was working out in my building. Girl, he still looks fine." Rachel told Allana with a thoughtful look on her face.

"So what has he been up to?"

"I don't know. You know how he used to be a clown and always telling jokes? Well, there was none of that, even in the short time we were talking. He has changed. I could see it in his eyes. We are having dinner this evening."

"Well, what do you think? Is he married or what?"

"Allana, we just spoke for a few minutes. I did notice there was no ring on his finger or tan lines that indicated there had been one. We will talk and catch up at dinner."

"I remember you two were always together. You were headed to the altar after graduation. Do you regret that the marriage did not happen?"

"For a while I was hurt. I loved James and wanted to spend the rest of my life with him. Things happen and eventually I moved on. It was hard no doubt, but I had to get it together and move toward my goals and dreams."

"Does he live here in Atlanta now?"

"No. He says he is here for some type of Minister's Conference. I'm not sure what that has to do with him, but he said he will be here at least until Friday of next week."

It was going on three o'clock and Rachel had some more errands to run before going home.

"Listen Allana, I still have a few more errands to run before dinner tonight. Would you like to have brunch tomorrow and maybe do some shopping?"

"Can we make it a late lunch or early dinner? I am going to church in the morning. Hey, why don't you come with me and we can just make a day of it. What do you say?"

"Can't you miss just one Sunday? I go back to work on Monday and we may not see each other again for a while."

"I could miss a Sunday but my day would feel incomplete if I don't go." Allana said.

"I don't think that would be a good idea. Besides I am upset with God right about now. I have been since high school graduation. As I said, I have done okay for myself and there is nothing we, God and I, have to say to each other." Rachel replied.

"Rachel, all I know is that no matter what you say or think God loves you. You may have issues with him but he does not have any issues with you. He is sad that you will no longer acknowledge him and realize that you need him.

"What don't you understand? I don't need him Allana. I think we better end this conversation. I'm not going and that is final." Rachel said in a huff.

Allana looked at her friend and was sad and hurt. She had to understand that all she could do was pray for her friend and let God do the rest.

"Well Rachel if that is how you feel. I will call you when I get out and see if we can get together. Remember friend that I love you, and I don't care what you say God loves you too."

"Whatever." Rachel said smugly.

While Allana was looking at her friend she was saying a silent prayer. She understands that while one does the planting and one does the watering, God does the increasing.

"Listen Rachel, I'm going to head back to the hotel. I do want us to get together tomorrow. If you change your mind about church just let me know ok."

"Allana I appreciate the offer but I will look for your call when you get out of church." Rachel gave her friend a look that said I doubt it.

With that they gave each other a hug. When they hugged Allana could feel the hurt that her friend was holding in. At that point she began to cry. Not loud but Rachel took notice when she sniffled.

"Allana, what's wrong? I'll call you tomorrow. Why are you crying?"

"You just don't understand how much you mean to me my forever friend. I just don't want anything to happen to you before you are able to accept Christ as your Savior." Allana told her.

Rachel stood back and just looked at her friend. She could not explain it but she saw a glow about her friend. Suddenly she felt overwhelmed with emotion. She wanted to cry but she refused to do so because that is not what she does. In her mind she felt she was just getting caught up with the emotions of her friend and refused to be sucked in like a little coward.

"Listen Allana, I appreciate your concern, really. But I am going to be just fine. Stop the blubbering and I promise I will call you tomorrow. I love you too friend for being so emotionally concerned for my well being. It's great that you have allowed God in your life but it's just not for me."

"It's not merely emotion that I felt when we were hugging. I felt the hurt that you carry with you daily and there is a solution to rid yourself of it but you won't even consider it."

"Allana, we'll talk about this another time okay. I really have to get going." Rachel told her while gathering her things to leave.

"Ok Rachel. I'll let it go for now. Just remember, you will deal with it now or you deal with it later, but you will have to deal with it. I mean everything that is keeping you from being truly happy on the inside."

Rachel put money on the table for her bill, turned and then started walking away. When the light changed for her to cross the street, out of nowhere she was pushed back up on the curb. Just as quickly, she noticed a car coming her way at a high rate of speed. The car had screeched in front of where she would have been walking, and kept going. Just as the car passed she looked at her friend who had just raised her head. When Allana had lifted her head Rachel had looked her way and saw the word Amen cross her lips. She felt the slight breeze of others walking past her and she realized the light had changed again. While walking to her car her mind was a whirl. She did not know what to think. That car was driving crazy. I could have been killed but something or someone moved me out of the way just in time. My friend was being honest when she said she was praying for me. They had been friends for a long time, yet she did not know this about her friend. Allana has always been a sensible and strong woman. Was she that weak that she needed a crutch to stand on? It just didn't make any sense.

Once Rachel reached her car she got in and just sat there. The tears that were trying to come out earlier started to fall. She began to wonder what the heck was going on. She does not get emotional about anything. There is no room for emotions in her life. As suddenly as the tears fell, that is how quickly she wiped her face and said, "Don't do this to yourself."

She put the key in the ignition then stopped short of turning the key in the ignition. Rachel jerked around like someone was in the car. She thought she heard a voice talking to her. After not seeing anything or anyone she turned the car on and headed toward home. There were still a few things she needed to do.

After pulling into her gated community, she headed toward the town portion to go to the grocery and the cleaners. She found a parking spot right in the middle of where she was trying to go. As Rachel parked the car she gathered her things. Just before she got out she thought she heard a voice again only this time it was a little louder. Climbing out of the car she looked around, hit the remote to lock it and started on her way. When she glanced at her watch she realized that she had plenty of time before dinner. It was such a nice day that she decided to be leisurely in her walk.

While strolling along the sidewalk she peeked through some of the windows along the way. She noticed the pet store had on display the cutest little dog. After stopping and looking the dogs over, she wondered if she should get herself a pet. Upon further consideration she decided that she just does not have the time. With working hectic hours there is no way she could properly take care of pet. Rachel kept walking and came upon Rayford's Cleaners and went in to retrieve her garments.

"Hello Miss Rachel. How are you today?" Calvin asked as he approached the counter.

"I'm doing well. I 'm just here to pick up my clothes, are they ready?" Rachel answered looking around.

"I just finished them about ten minutes ago. Let me get them for you. I'll be right back." Calvin said as he disappeared behind the clothes filled rack.

As Rachel was waiting for Calvin to return someone else came into the store. Just then Calvin came back with her clothes and hung them on the pole next to the counter. Rachel perused the plastic bag to ensure that all of her things were there. Once she was satisfied that they were she asked, "How much do I owe you?"

"That will be twenty five dollars."

Calvin told her.

Rachel pulled out her billfold and retrieved the money and handed it to Calvin. In turn he rang up the items and gave her a receipt.

"Thank you and come again." Calvin said to her as she picked up her items.

"Thank you." Rachel replied.

After adjusting the clothing on her arm she turned and walked out of the door. She started to continue on but decided to put the clothes in the car. While opening up the trunk of her car she felt as though someone was staring at her. She casually laid the clothes in the trunk and glanced around to see if she noticed anyone looking at her. It turns out it there was no one around. Rachel closed the trunk and went about her way to finish her errands.

In her mind she was thinking about the conversation she had at the restaurant with her friend. She was thinking about how she had talked to her friend throughout the year and Allana had not said anything to her about getting religious. To be honest, she thought, their conversations were different. They were not the same kidding and gossiping as it used to be. We used to talk bad about people and dog them out, but over the year the conversations have been more peaceful. Whatever she does is her business. I have been doing fine and I will continue to do fine. Leaning on God is just a crutch for the weak. Besides, I am the one who went to school. I busted my butt to make sure that I got my degree one year ahead of schedule.

Why am I wasting my thoughts on this subject because it is a done deal? While she walked she encountered a florist with plants lining the front of the store. She decided to pick out a few for her living room and dining room tables as centerpieces. After picking the flowers she went inside the store to pay for them. The cashier thanked her and said something that made Rachel stop in her tracks.

"God bless you and have a great day." That is what the cashier said, but what Rachel actually heard was "I love you." She turned and looked at the cashier with fire in her eyes and said,

"What do you mean you love me? I don't know you."

"Excuse me" the cashier said.

"I said, why did you tell me you love

me?"

"I did not say that. I said God bless you

and have a great day."

"Oh. I'm sorry. I've had kind of a rough

start today."

"We'll, pray things will get better. Is

there anything else I can help you with?"

"No thank you."

With that Rachel walked quickly out the

florist shop and headed to the car. Once she put

the flowers in the backseat on the floor she

headed home. She needed to get home to settle

down before meeting James this evening. When

Rachel arrived home she went straight to her

condo. She made nice with nobody. There is

too much going on and she needed to lie down.

Rachel went to the bedroom to hang her clothes

and then came to the kitchen to put the flowers in water. As she looked for the vases to put the flowers in she noticed a message on the answering machine. She hit the button and listened.

"Ms. Abney, this is Frank at the front desk. A gentleman by the name of James Rivers left a message stating he will be a little late and to expect him around eight o'clock. He apologizes for the inconvenience but was unable to call you himself because he had no other way to get in touch with you." Rachel stopped the machine.

With that information she looked at her watch and decided she had time to take a shower and take a nap. The day started off well but has ended in confusion and a bit stressful. "I am not going to stress over this anymore" She said to herself. Rachel finished arranging the flowers and headed toward the bedroom. Before she started the water she chose another CD to put in the player in the bathroom. This time she opted for old school and chose Marvin Gaye. She thought how he was a man ahead of his time. If he were living today he would be off the chain. The youngsters wouldn't be able to touch him.

Rachel started the water and got it as hot as she could stand it. While letting the water run down her back she went over the days events. Why did she get mad at her friend she wondered? It really did not matter at this point. What is done is done. She will be ok. Besides this does not concern me she thought. Rachel washed herself then got out of the shower. She ended up putting on her undergarments so she would not have that much to do when it was time to get ready.

She stretched out across the bed and immediately drifted to sleep. As she entered the dream state of her sleep she started to stir. Rachel was thinking of what Allana had told her about how God loved her and died for her. Just then a bloody figure stood before her and looked at her. Rachel began to shift in her sleep as though she was frightened by the body standing before her. Knowing she should be afraid she was not. The look on the man's face was one of peace. The look in the man's eyes was one of love. His hair was bloodied and matted, face was beaten and bruised.

When she began to look at him more closely she noticed a scar on his side like someone had poked a hole there. There was blood and water coming from that wound but the person never said a word. There was blood coming from his hands and feet. Rachel's facial expression while sleeping had a horrified look of pity. She could not say a word and all she could do was stare in amazement of the torture this poor man had endured. The real question in her mind was why was he standing in front of her? Rachel began to wonder if she knew this man. The man lifted his hands as if wanting to hold her and Rachel jumped up in her bed.

Rachel looked around in astonishment. She was drenched in a cold sweat. She looked at the clock and noticed it was seven fifteen and she needed to start getting ready. Before she moved to get up, she wiped her face with her hands then settled her face in them. Going over the events in the dream she shuddered at the thought and looked at her own hands as though she was going to see the hands of the man in her dream. She sat on the edge of the bed for a few seconds then got up. Rachel went to the bathroom to retrieve a towel to thoroughly wipe her face of the perspiration.

Once she completed that task she looked into the mirror. Her face looked a little weary but she figured once she had a glass of wine while dressing she will be alright. After getting dressed she went into the living room and sat on the sofa. It was now seven fifty-five. She thought she would go ahead and wait for James downstairs since he did not know where she lived in the building. By the time she gathered her purse, keys and jacket it was eight o'clock. She got on the elevator and noticed a different person manning the controls. The name tagged read "Nate".

"Good evening Ma'am."

"Good evening Nate. Have I ever seen you before tonight?"

"No Ma'am. I have only been here a couple of weeks. I work evenings and some weekends. I usually come on when you are already home and gone by the time you leave in the mornings."

"Well, welcome to the building."

"Thank you. Here you go. Have a good evening" Nate said.

"You have a good evening also. Maybe we will run into each other again."

The elevators closed and Nate was on his way to his next destination. Rachel looked around to see if she could spot James.

Unfortunately he was nowhere around. She decided to take a seat facing the door as to not miss him when he came in. Looking at her watch she noticed it was five after eight. Before she sat down she walked to the front desk to make sure there were no messages. To her surprise there weren't any. As she settled in the chair she took the time to notice how beautiful the lobby was decorated. Because she had been so busy lately all she did was go to work, come home, sleep and start the process all over again without paying attention to the small things of where she lived.

In the cab on his way back to condo, James was thinking how excited he was having seen Rachel again. Running into her at the exercise room, he believes, was not coincidental. He chuckled at himself when he noticed Rachel checking him out. Only at that time he did not know it was her. Once he started lifting barbells he realized that it was Rachel. He continued his repetition on the barbells and noticed her trying to be coy about her checking him out. He thought how she still looked as good as she did when they last saw each other. As a matter of fact, she looked fantastic.

The smile melted as he remembered how hurt she looked when he told her that he joined the service. It was a choice that he decided to take without talking to her first. At that time in my life, he thought, was the time for him to serve his country while pursuing his education. I just assumed Rachel would wait because she loved me. I gambled and lost. Well she seems to have gone on with her life okay and seems to be doing well in her chosen profession. The only thing is that even though I married she did not make me as happy as Rachel.

It did not last and I have been single every since. As the cab came upon the condo building where his friend was staying he checked his watch. It was eight twenty-five. I hope she will still agree to have dinner or go for coffee. He paid the cab and the door was opened by the doorman. He got out of the cab in a hurry and rushed into the building. He looked around in angst and noticed Rachel sitting in the chair with a grim look on her face.

"Rachel, I am so sorry for being late. I thought I would've been here by now but the afternoon meeting started late, and then of course ended later than I had anticipated. Have you been down here long?"

"No, not really, but it is getting too late to be going out to eat." Rachel said in that tone that only he recognizes.

"Well, would you at least join me for a cup of coffee? There is so much we need to catch up on. There is so much I need to tell you. What do you say?"

Rachel looked at him and just thought how handsome he looked in that suit.

"James, I have really had a rough day. Let's go up to my place and talk."

James was surprised by the offer but decided what the heck.

"Ok." James replied grinning.

"What are you grinning about? This is not what you think it is or will turn out to be mister man" she said smiling.

"Whatever do you mean? We are just going to have coffee, but I would rather have tea, talk and catch up on old times. What's the harm in that?"

"I just wanted you to be perfectly clear."

As Rachel arose from her chair, James extended his hand to give assistance. She hesitated then placed her hand in his and stood without letting go of his hand. Once she was situated and began to take a step she tried to let go of his hand and realized James was not going to let it go. Because he was not holding it tight she decided to pull a little harder without being overtly obvious. With that James let go of her hand and they continued to walk toward the elevator.

When the elevator arrived, Maurice was the operator and said, "Good evening Ma'am, Sir."

"Good evening they both said in unison."

With that the door closed and they road to Rachel's floor in silence. The only sound was that of the music piped into the elevator car. Once they reached Rachel's floor they stepped off the elevator and Rachel reached in her purse to retrieve her keys. As she was searching for her keys, James just stared at her in awe of how beautiful she is. This is the woman he fell in love with so many years ago and broke her heart. "How could I be so selfish?" he thought. He shook his head to come back to the present. He understands that in order to be in the place he is in today that he had to leave her back then.

Just then Rachel found her keys and unlocked the door. As he follows her into the condo, she flicks on a wall switch. The place is illuminated with a lighted chandelier in the middle of the living room.

"Welcome to my humble abode," Rachel says to James as she opens her arms and waves them across the room.

"This is beautiful Rachel. It looks just like you. You did a great job decorating." James replied.

"I would love to take credit but I can't. My work schedule picked up quickly and I had to hire a decorator. All I did was tell them what I was looking for and they did the rest."

"Well they did a great job."

"Can I get you something to drink? I have wine, wine cooler, tea, and water."

"I'll have tea, thank you. Hot if it won't be any trouble."

"No trouble at all. I'll put the water on to boil. Will you excuse me while I get into something a little bit more comfortable?"

"Sure, go ahead. I'm not going anywhere." James said following her with his eyes.

Rachel removes her dress and high heel shoes. She decides to put on a pair of slacks, pullover sweater, and her slippers. Afterwards she looked in the mirror, refreshed her makeup and by this time the whistle began to sound so she headed into the kitchen. She notices James looking around and without noticing her he sits on the sofa and makes himself comfortable. As he sits on the sofa in front of the fireplace he starts to stare at a picture hanging on the wall above it. He noticed it was a picture by the famed artist Thomas Kincaid. It was sunset over the beach scene with vibrant evening colors depicting the sky, ocean and beach. Just then Rachel came into the room.

James stood as any gentleman would when a woman entered the room and helped her with the tray of beverages. Once he placed the tray on the table he hesitated before sitting down waiting on Rachel to take a seat first.

"Would you like sugar or honey with your tea?" Rachel asked.

"I'll take honey."

Rachel began to pour the tea and gave it and the honey to James.

"Would you like a lemon wedge?"

"Yes." was James' reply.

Rachel poured herself a cup of tea with honey and lemon, and sat back on the couch and took a careful sip because the tea was extremely hot.

"So," Rachel began. "How have you been?"

"Things have been good. I apologize again about tonight. I had a meeting that was scheduled to start at one time and ended up starting one hour later. You know how your people are." James said with a chuckle.

"Now why do they have to be my people?" Rachel said with a sarcastic tone and laughter.

"You know what I'm saying. If you want us to be somewhere on time to do something, just tell them an hour later than the actual time and then they will be on time." James said.

They both broke out into a roar of laughter.

"To be honest, unfortunately that is right." Rachel said smiling.

"No really, I had to attend to this business so I could spend the rest of my time as I saw fit. How have you been doing? It has been a really long time since we've seen each other. I have missed you something terrible. You were not only my girlfriend but you were my best friend."

Rachel glanced up while sipping on her tea. When she looked into his eyes, she remembered how beautiful they were. There was the sincerity that she had forgotten about James. After putting the cup back on the table she just looked afar off as if to journey to a distant place in her past.

"I've been good. As with anybody's life there have been some ups and downs but overall I have been doing pretty well. You know the routine. I go to work, come home and go out occasionally. On the rare occasion that I am able to relax, I go shopping. As you noticed today I definitely workout every chance I get. I'm living to survive, nothing more." Rachel responded.

James was looking at her while she talked. He thought how she has taken care of herself over the years. She looks good.

"That's good. There have been some changes for me over the years as well. As I said earlier these are changes that I want to tell you about." James said.

Rachel started scanning his face. She could detect something that she could not put her finger. This was definitely not the same man she fell in love with over twenty years ago.

"Yeah, I remember you telling me about bootlegging as a preacher. "What's up with that?"

"Again, I am not bootlegging. I know when we were young we went to church because we were forced to by our parents. But it was not until I enlisted in the Army that I realized that I needed a personal relationship with God."

"Come on James, you too?" Rachel said exasperated.

"What do you mean 'you too'?

"Do you remember my best friend Allana Majors?"

"Of course I do. When you were not with me you were with her. You two were as thick as thieves. How is she doing these days?"

"She's doing okay. Anyway, that is who I had lunch with today. She told me that she gave her life to God. We talk all the time but she felt she had to come to Atlanta to tell me this instead of over the phone."

"That is great news. Why do you sound as though you don't want to hear this?"

"I'm sorry. It has been a long day. Go ahead and tell me your story. Since God has been the headlining feature for the day, you might as well give me the details of your story."

"Why are you being cynical? This isn't like you."

"Well a lot has changed since you made the decision to leave me after graduation."

"Are you still angry about that? I thought you understood. The way my life turned out it was the best decision I made. That decision has made me the man I am today."

"The best decision for you maybe. I went through hell trying to get over you. After that things were just not the same. I felt abandoned by you. Forget it because I have."

"Evidently not because you just threw it up in my face. You have been holding on this for twenty years. Believe me when I tell you that I never wanted to hurt you. I loved you but needed to grow up and find out who James Rivers was and what he had to offer the world."

"While you were off trying figure out who the hell you were, I was being miserable and feeling like I had nothing to offer the world. But that only lasted for about six months."

"So you were able to forget me after just six months?"

"No. But in order for me to move on I had to put you out my mind and heart. Trust me, as painful as it was to do, I did it."

"Well I'm glad to know that you could move on so quickly." He said very sarcastically. Then he said, "I'm sorry for that last remark."

"Oh, it's okay. I didn't mean to go off like that. Please continue with what you were saying before I took a left turn."

"You have every right to go to the left or right. I hurt you and we never talked about it after the decision to go our separate ways was made. Right now I want to go on record and say that I am sorry for hurting you the way I did. I loved you then and I still care about you."

"James, you just don't know all that I have been through. The love I had for you was like no other. You were the only one from grade school through high school."

"After boot camp I was able to go to town on leave. I met girls everywhere I went, but no one compared to you. After a while I began to numb the pain of leaving you with alcohol. Shortly after boot camp we were deployed to the Persian Gulf for the war that took place. When I enlisted in the military there was no threat of war. I figured I could go to school on the military's dime and see the world. A year later all of that changed when the Gulf War started."

"But James, you had a full ride to any college you wanted to attend. You could've written your own ticket to see the world. Why did you feel you needed to go away from here, away from me?"

"Why do you keep saying 'away from you'? I never wanted to leave you."

"For someone who never wanted to leave you sure didn't mind doing and exit stage left."

"Rachel, what I did was for the both of us. My thought was to go to the military, get a degree, find a good job and then send for you. Once I started dating other women I felt that I could not return to you so I just kept moving."

"Whatever. So finish what you were saying."

"Like I said, I used alcohol to numb the pain of not being with you. I slept around and fell in love, or what I thought was love. The next thing I knew I was married. That woman was crazy. She was the sweetest thing while we were dating, but as soon as we said 'I do' the real person came out. Six months into the marriage her mother, sister and her sister's three kids were living with us in a two bedroom house. I would not have minded if we had discussed it, but she made the decision and basically told me that was the way it was going to be."

"Why didn't you put your foot down?"

"I couldn't because she was standing on both of them."

"What did you do?"

"The only thing I could do at the time. I went to work, paid the bills and found reasons to stay away. I found no need to come home because her mother had taken over every aspect of my house but the bedroom. After eight months of marriage that area went out the window."

"There would be no way that I would allow that to happen to me. My mother in-law would not take over."

"Well it all came to a boiling point one night when I got home. Her mother started in on me about not doing my fair share of the household duties. I listened to her and could not believe she would have the nerve to talk to me like I was a ten year old that did not do his chores. The more she talked the more upset I became. I'm thinking, this woman has invaded my home six months into my marriage, and has taken over everything from cooking to telling my wife how to deal with me."

"Just how mad did you actually get?"

James looked at her and smiled and said "As mad as a volcano that was about to explode. And when she made a comment about not spending enough alone time with my wife the volcano blew. I went to the jugular of her neck, grab it and yanked her forward."

Rachel's eyes grew big and she put her hands up to her mouth. Once she settled herself she said "James you didn't kill her did you?"

"No, but believe me when I say that I really wanted to. Before I yanked her neck again I let her go. She looked at me in horror then she slapped me. I was caught off guard and stumbled backward. Once I regained my composure I told her to pack her bags and get out taking her other daughter and her children with her."

"Then what happened?"

"She walked up to me and looked me straight in the eyes and said that she was not going anywhere. I told her she was sadly mistaken and told her to be gone by the time I returned home and if she was not gone I would call the police. I left the house and went to the neighborhood tavern and had a couple of drinks giving her time to get her stuff together and leave."

Just then Rachel interrupted him before he went on and said "I'm getting hungry, would you like me to order a pizza or fix you a sandwich?"

"That would be great. I am getting a little hungry myself. Let's order a pizza. Whatever you want is fine. Could you get some chicken wings and breadsticks with cheese sauce?"

"Are you sure you are just a little hungry?" Rachel asked smirking.

"Don't worry, I'll pay for it."

"I'm not worried. That was a given." After placing the pizza order, Rachel went to the living room to retrieve the tea cups and asked James if he would like some more.

"No. May I have some water instead?"

"Sure."

Rachel went back into the kitchen and returned with a bottle of water for James and a wine cooler for herself. She handed him the water and then sat back down on her end of the sofa. When he opened the water and started to drink, Rachel just looked at him and wondered who this guy was. She knew it was James but like earlier she knew something was different. When he stopped drinking, she quickly diverted her eyes to keep from being conspicuous about staring at him.

"So you were saying? What happened next?"

"Well, needless to say that when I got home she was still there. Not only that, my wife, her sister and the children had come back home. As soon as I stepped in the door Kayla, my wife, jumped up in my face and started in on me about choking her mother and ordering her to leave."

"You do not put your hands on my mother or tell her what to do. And by the way, you answer to me and not the other way around." Kayla had said.

"Now keep in mind that I had a few drinks but I was not drunk, just buzzing. I stood there and looked at her then at her mother.

Although I wanted to handle this situation in a very different way, I just walked passed both of them and went into our bedroom. She tried to come after me but I slammed the door in her face before she got there. She was not happy about that at all. So she could not get in I put a chair that was in the room under the doorknob. She was on the other side of the door screaming and banging on it like there was a fire."

"What were you doing?"

"I was pacing the floor and thinking. I had no idea what to do or what I wanted to do. All I knew was that this could not continue the way it was going. Something had to change or someone was going to get hurt. After about ten minutes she stopped her antics. Five minutes later I went into the living room. They looked at me with fire in their eyes and started to speak but I sternly looked back and they stopped in mid sentence. For the first time I felt like I was in control."

Just then the doorbell rang and it was the pizza delivery. James reached in his pocket for his wallet and paid for the food. He followed Rachel into the kitchen and put the food on the counter. He stood there as she reached for the plates. James admired her and thought how he wished he had done right by her. If he had they would be married with a couple of kids of their own.

"Here, let me help you with that" James said.

Rachel stepped back and watched as he reached for the plates. Looking at him as he pulled the plates from the shelf, all she could think was that she needed another drink. It was starting to get a little warm as she smiled to herself. Just then James turned around and accidentally bumped into her.

"Sorry about that" he said.

"That's okay. I guess I was standing a little too close."

Rachel grabbed the pizza, retrieved the paper towels, and then headed toward the living room. "Will you grab the wings? The ranch dressing is in the refrigerator. Feel free to grab a drink and will you bring me a wine cooler? Thank you."

As they started to settle down they each reached for a slice of the pizza as well as a couple of chicken wings. They both ate in silence. Once a couple of bites were taken by each, they sat back on the couch.

"I guess I was hungrier than I thought"
Rachel said with a sigh.

"I just realized that I haven't had
anything really tangible since breakfast. I've
been snacking all day." James added
James took a swig of his water as Rachel took a
sip of her wine cooler.

"Now that was tasty. Can I get you
anything else?" Rachel asked.

"No thank you. I'm going to let this sit
for a minute before I dig back in. That pizza is
great."

"You think so? Actually this is the first
time I've tried it. It tasted okay. I like the
wings. So, you need to finish telling me what
happened. It sounds like you had started getting
your say."

"Oh. Well, like I said something had to change or there was going to be blood shed. I told her mother that she was no longer welcome in my house and she must leave immediately taking her daughter and children with her. She tried to protest and I stood my ground."

"I know your wife was furious. What did she do?"

"She tried to get loud and started pointing her finger in my face about how her mother and sister were not going anywhere. I told her as a matter of fact that she was free to leave also. Keeping in mind that if she left she better take everything because there was no coming back to retrieve anything."

"Oooohhh. What happened then?"

"My wonderful wife decided that she would let her mother go and stay with me. She says that standing up to her was kind of sexy. I thought that she was nuts and decided that I no longer wanted the headache.

"You didn't?"

"I did. I told her to get her stuff and get out. She started crying and apologizing for everything. I was sorry too, for taking too long to see that I married her for the wrong reasons. I was sorry that I allowed myself to waste so much time in a dead end relationship. I went to the courthouse the next day and filed for divorce."

"I'm sorry that you had to go there but glad that you are okay."

"I'm just fine. I am waiting on the Lord to send me my queen and when He does I will do things the right way."

"Why do you think God will have anything to do with who you marry? Or do anything else for that matter." Rachel asked half sarcastically.

"Everything that concerns me concerns him. He loves me that much."

"How you figure that? What has he done for you lately?"

"For one thing he let me live another day."

"So what is that suppose to mean. We were going to wake up anyway."

"Let me finish the story and maybe you will understand better."

"I doubt it but go ahead."

"Well, while going through the divorce proceedings my drinking became increasingly worse. I became depressed and suicidal because

I did not see a future for me. Although I went to school while in the military, I could not find a job in my profession when I was discharged. I realized that a diploma or degree means nothing in these economic times."

"I have managed to keep my job. I do quite nicely if I do say so for myself."

"And you don't see how that it is a blessing from the Almighty God?

"No. I have worked hard to get to where I am today. I hope to make partner by this time next year."

"Rachel. What happened to all the teachings we received in Sunday school when we were young?"

"You said it. We were young and believed whatever we were told. I do not need structured religion telling me who to serve and how to act. I find it to be a bunch of bull."

"Anyway, while moving from job to job I was able to start over and became the manager for a popular eating establishment. My immediate boss was a Christian. He was not a man of many words but he showed his love of Christ by what he did. He started inviting me to church. It was possible to do that because his establishment was closed on Sunday's. I was giving him excuse after excuse until he stopped asking. You see, I did not feel that I could go to church in the shape I was in. I still drank and had started smoking pot. I was at a party and someone wanted me to take a hit of cocaine. That was where I drew the line."

"James, I had no idea you were in such a state."

"How could you know? When I was discharged from the service you had already moved out of town. I only stayed with my parents for a hot minute."

"But once you found out where I was why, didn't you look me up?"

"Because, I was a mess and did not want you to see me that way. Besides you had already moved on with some other guy."

"How do you know that?" Rachel asked, trying to conceal the pained expression on her face.

"I did some digging when I got back. I also heard you were going to get married. What happened with that?"

Rachel picked up her drink, and while staring into a far away place, started to swirl the bottle. She was trying to decide whether she wanted to travel this road. After a couple of quick swirls she took a big gulp and decided that she was not ready to talk about that just yet. After swallowing the drink and letting it marinate in her belly for what seemed to be forever she finally said, "It just didn't happen. I really don't feel like talking about it."

"Will you ever tell me what happened?"

"I doubt it. Don't hold your breath. Now finish your story."

"That's not fair." James said smiling.

"Well, that is the way it will have to be. You can finish or you can leave. Take your pick."

"Since I have stumbled upon a touchy subject, I will let this pass and finish."

"Thank you." Rachel said with a slight grin easing on her lips.

"Anyway, some time had passed before my boss asked me again to go to church. I will never forget it because it was then that I decided to take him up on his offer. It was Easter Sunday. The name of the Church was "Always the Truth of God". The church did not have a large congregation, maybe one hundred or one hundred-fifty members. What I did not know was that my boss was the head deacon in his church and well respected. The people were gathering for morning service right after Sunday school.

We found a seat toward the middle and sat down. The choir was great and really set the tone for the rest of the service. The pastor, Bishop Morris E. W. Gates came to the podium and welcomed everyone before beginning his sermon. The thing was that while he was preaching there were people acting out different scenes from his sermon. He was talking about the birth, death, burial and resurrection of Jesus. It was awesome."

"Come on James. Were you at a church service or a play? Who does that anyway?"

"Listen Rachel, I was at church. It is one thing to read about stuff, it is a whole other ball game to see it play out right in front of you."

"What was the catch? I'm sure they asked for money once the performance was done. That's how they get you. They tell you it is free then once you get in the door they ask for a donation of a specific amount of money. Besides, how can you put an amount on a donation?"

"You are something else you know that? There was no charge before, during or after. I was listening so intently I felt as if the pastor was talking directly to me."

"There were others in that church, so what made you feel so important?"

"I don't know? The pastor was talking about how Jesus was born to take away the sins of the world. He was also saying that no matter what we do he loves us. When it came to the part about Jesus being killed on the cross, I felt like I was there. I felt like if I had been the only person He would have died just for me."

"You have got to be kidding. You actually believe that stuff?"

"You did to at one time." James said with a slightly agitated voice.

"Well I'm all grown up now and that kind of brainwashing is not necessary." Rachel snapped back.

James looked at his watch and realized it was getting late.

"Rachel, it's getting late and I don't want to over stay my welcome. I'm going to be in town for at least another few days. Can we finish this another time?" James said, reaching for his water.

"You will not leave me hanging like this. Besides, I have plans tomorrow and I go back to work on Monday to start a new project."

"Okay then. What it boils down to is that I gave my life to Jesus Christ. I have been saved for five years now. After the vivid picture that I saw of Christ, I decided to stop playing stupid and start walking out my destiny, serving him. You see, every one of us was created to worship him and live for him. When he comes again for his church, after a period of time we will stand before him and be judged for our actions and decisions while we were here on earth."

"What do you mean when he comes back? You just said that he was killed."

"Jesus Christ is coming back for a church without spot or blemish. We are not perfect and never will be. But what is important is to accept Jesus as Lord and Savior, be baptized in Jesus Name and He will give you the Holy Ghost with evidence of speaking in tongues. This is a heavenly language that is given to the believer. I know this is a lot to take in right now."

"I'm not taking it in at all. You are talking crazy. There is no way I am going to believe this stuff. Sounds like you got yourself hooked up in some kind of cult. Is this Jim Jones' cousin?" Rachel asked laughing. James looked at Rachel with pity in his eyes.

"Do you really think I would get involved in something like that? All I know is God loves me. I gave my life to him to serve him while on earth to dwell with him forever in heaven. God loves you too and want you to experience his unconditional love as well."

"Like I said before, I have everything I want. I have no need to trust in a God that may or may not exist. I have no need to use a fabricated, fairy tale entity as a crutch for my being alive. Thanks, but no thanks." Rachel said as she stood and walked toward the patio.

"I want you to understand that all you have and own can be taken from you at anytime. Everything you have worked for means nothing to God. The only thing God wants is your soul. It belongs to him anyway. He just wants you to give it back to him freely."

As Rachel looked out of the patio she started to get upset. First it was her friend Allana, and now James. What in the world is going on? Then she heard something. It was faint but clear-I Love you.

"What did you say?" She asked James.

"I said God just wants you to give yourself to him freely."

"No. What did you say after that?"

"I didn't say anything."

"Yes you did. You said you loved me."

"No I didn't. You're hearing things."

Rachel's wall clock chimed and she noticed that it was one o'clock in the morning.

"Listen, it is getting late. Maybe you should leave now."

"Look Rachel, why don't you come to church with me and hear the word for yourself." James said as he stood and made his way toward Rachel.

"No. You and Allana have lost your mind. Now that you both have gone God crazy you are trying to hook me and I won't stand for it." Rachel declared defiantly.

James stared at Rachel with disbelief at what she was saying. As he turned to head toward the door he stopped in his tracks as if he were being blocked from going any further. He bowed his head and then turned back toward Rachel.

"Before I go I just want you to know something. Jesus is coming back real soon. You say you do not believe there is a God and that's okay because I know you know different. You have been hurt and believe that God is the reason so you refuse to trust anyone else, especially him. Well just keep this in mind. If you do not accept him into your heart and live for him as best you can by his Word, you will not reign with him. You will be sentenced to a life of misery in hell. God does not send people to hell their decisions send them to hell. Rachel, I care about you and want you to be happy."

"James, I am happy. I have everything I need or want." Rachel replied.

"Superficially you may be happy because of stuff and things. True happiness comes from having a real personal relationship with Jesus Christ."

"Yeah? Where was "God" when you left me? Where was he when I thought I found love again and this joker was snorting coke up his nose? Where was "God Almighty" when I lost my baby? If you can answer those questions then I may be able to digest what you are telling me." Rachel said with disdain and anger in her voice.

"Rachel, I am sorry for everything that you have been through. Believe me when I say that I would not wish those things on anybody. What you need to understand is that everything you have been through up to this point, God has been right there with you." James tried to explain.

"I tell you what, why don't you just leave and take your new found faith in God with you. Matter of fact I do not wish to hear any more about it." Rachel said walking toward the door.

James headed toward the door and turned to her and was getting ready to say something when Rachel interrupted.

"I would appreciate it if you not contact me again. Enjoy your stay here in Atlanta."

"What are you talking about?"

"I'm talking about you not calling me. I get this feeling that every time we see each other you are going to want to talk about God. To keep from being rude I just assume you do not call me."

"Come on Rachel, there is more to me than that. We can have lunch or you can take me sightseeing while I'm in town."

Rachel had her hand on the doorknob and hesitated for a second and then said, "I'll see. Goodnight."

James smiled and walked out of the door.

Before Rachel closed the door he managed to be able to say, "I'll see you in a couple of days."

With that Rachel closed the door. Sighing heavily she leaned against the door. After what seemed to be forever she moved toward the living room and started gathering up the remainder of the food and dishes and put them in the kitchen. She put the food in the refrigerator, loaded the dishwasher and turned it on. Rachel was feeling a little stressed by the conversation so she grabbed the bottle of wine

and poured herself a glass and took a long gulp.
She refilled the glass and headed toward the
bedroom.

Rachel decided that this had been a very
tiring day with all the conversation about God.
After putting on her night clothes she went into
the living room and closed the vertical blinds
leading to the patio and turned off the lights.
Trudging to the bedroom she sat on the end of
her bed. Then out of no where she heard again
what she had been hearing all day- I love you.
She shook it off, took one more drink of wine
and climbed into bed.

Meanwhile, James had returned to the
condo where he was staying. He was tired and
sad. He was tired because of a long day and sad
because of the conversation with Rachel. As he

began to prepare for bed he stopped and started to pray.

"Father, I thank you for being the creator of all heaven and earth. Thank you for your promise of your return, and for helping us to get to the point of asking that your will be done in our lives. I come not on my own behalf but on behalf of your daughter Rachel. Lord, she has hardened her heart and appears to not want to allow you to enter in. You know all things and you also know those who will accept you and live for you as well as those who will reject you.

"Lord, I pray this night that you continue to send people her way to help guide her heart toward you. Satan, the Lord rebukes your attempts to keep this soul from the light of God's truth. In Jesus Name, she will accept the

Lord as her Savior and His grace toward her. She will live out the rest of her life giving God the glory and praise. In Jesus name she will be a witness to your people. Lord, thank you in advance for your divine will being done in her life. Thank you for using me in whatever capacity that is necessary to spread your word, not only to Rachel but fulfilling your call on my life to the nations and the world. I praise you because you are worthy. I thank you for saving me from a life destined for eternal hell. Forever will I serve you and bless your name. Continue to strengthen me for thy service. In Jesus' Name, Amen."

After ending his prayer James went into the bathroom and brushed his teeth. Once he completed that task he returned to the room and pulled back the covers so he could get in. As he made preparation to retire for the evening he picked up his bible and started reading. This is a habit that he has developed over the years. He feels that going to sleep after reading the word will help him not only sleep better but think on the things of God while he is asleep.

Back at Rachel's, she has finally slipped into a coma like state of sleep. The fact that she has had several wine coolers has helped intensify the sleep process. In her sleep state she began to stir. The pictures going through her mind were the different conversations from her friends Allana and James. She rolled to the other side of her bed still totally immersed in her sleep. Rachel began to drift even deeper into her slumber. She found herself standing before a white throne. There were hundreds of millions of people all around her. The place

surrounding her was illuminated with endless
rays of bright light. She looked around in
amazement wondering what type of place this
was.

Rachel tried to speak but could not utter
a word. She observed the one sitting on the
white throne had two books. As she looked
around she was curious as to what was about to
happen. Suddenly one by one the names of
those standing around were being called.
Rachel was amazed at the orderliness of all of
people. When the names were called those that
were even as far back as you could not see
heard their names. There were no megaphones,
microphones or even a loudspeaker system.
The one calling out the names spoke in a normal
tone, but the voice was gentle, loving and soft.

Because she was up front she was able to hear what was being said for each person coming forth. One person was told that they lived and exemplary life of faith once she gave her life over to her creator, in which he was speaking of himself. He also told her that things were hard for her raising here two daughters alone but no matter what she prayed and did not stray or give up; especially when she found out her daughter said she was living a lifestyle that was against his Word.

It suddenly dawned on Rachel where she was and who was doing the talking. She realized she was in heaven in the presence of God. As she stood there, her mouth was hanging open in awe. When she was young she heard the stories but she thought that was all they were. As she focused her attention back on

the women standing before God she noticed the
lady was crying. God told her to wipe her tears.
Because of her faithfulness she would reign
with him forever. He also told her that because
of her prayers and the life she lived before her
daughter, she also re-committed her life back to
him bringing her friends and others in the
homosexual and lesbian lifestyle to a saving
knowledge of him. They had lived the rest of
their lives spreading his Word and helping
others get delivered from the lies of Satan. Now
go, worship me forever.

Rachel was excited for her and all the
others that had come forth who were told of
their life in Christ. Then there was a man that
came forth after his name was called. God
looked into another book and started reading off
the deeds of this man. It read like a resume of

all he accomplished and the amount of money he had accumulated over the years prior to his death. I was impressed but the look on God's face was one of disappointment. The conversation went like this.

"I see where you worked hard all of your life and amassed a great fortune."

"I had to. My family was poor when I was growing up and I was determined that poverty would not be my lot in life."

"I also see where you had a wife, three children and a mistress with a son by her. Do you think that was the right thing to do?"

"Well, my wife, all she wanted to do was go to church and give my money to them. On top of all of that she would tell me that it could be taken away at any time so I decided to stay because of the laws regarding alimony."

"I see. What about the example you set for your two sons and daughter? Your actions have caused your sons to treat women the way you treated your wife, and your daughter? Well, lets just say that your daughter has been looking for the approval of a man all of her life because she did not get the kind of support and nurturing from you she needed."

"I bought my children everything they ever wanted. They had no need for anything."

"They needed you to be the man of God your wife had prayed for. They needed for you to teach them what it meant to honor marriage vows, to help those less fortunate, to live for me instead of your money and other women."

"I did toward the end of my life. I tried to make up for the wrong I had done. Doesn't that count for something?"

"It would if you had confessed a belief in me and made me Lord and Savior of your life. Everything you have I gave you. I gave you the mind to make money and succeed in the business aspect of your life. I gave you a family and you failed at that. When you had the chance to make it right, you did but not according to my Word. Because of this I must banish you to death to spend eternity in the lake of fire."

"But Lord, please don't send me there. I am sorry for everything. Please give me a second chance to do this right. Give me a chance to make things right with my children and wife."

"Depart from me. I know you not."

With that the man disappeared. God was sad but He knew it had to be done. It appeared to take a long time calling each name because of the multitude, but it didn't. Rachel looked around and saw that she was the only one standing. God looked at her and looked into the book of life and did not see her name. After flipping through the pages of the book of life, He turned his attention to the other book. Looking at the book and what she had done, he looked at her. Because of the look in his eyes, Rachel had a horrified look on her face. She thought there would be no way she would go the way of the lake.

God must know that I am a good person. I am not like that one guy. I made a fortune but helped people in need. I gave to charities, gave generous bonuses to my people on my job. She thought about the other guy and remembered that his good deeds did not do him any good.

The very thing he did not do she realized she hadn't done it either. Just before God began to speak Rachel let out a scream and started yelling. "I will not go. I can't go to hell for eternity. There must be something I can do. Please God give me another chance to get it right."

Just then Rachel lurched forward in her bed. She was breathing hard and drenched in a cold sweat. She looked around in horror trying to get her bearings as to where she was. Once she realized she was home in her bed she moved to the edge of the bed and just sat there. "I have to stop drinking so much before I go to sleep. Alcohol will make you dream some crazy stuff." Just then she heard what sounded like a voice say—but I love you. She jerked around to see where it was coming from, but she did not see anything or anyone in the darkness of her room. Rachel struggled to her feet and made her way to the bathroom. She turned on the light and looked into the mirror. Looking at herself in the mirror she noticed the worn look on her face. "I didn't know I look this bad in the middle of the night." she chuckled to herself. Once she washed her face and changed her nightclothes she went into the kitchen. She looked at the clock and saw that it was only six o'clock in the morning. While looking in the refrigerator she started to grab the wine cooler but changed her mind and decided to have a cup of hot tea instead. After putting on the water to boil she went to the door to see if the Sunday newspaper had arrived. Once she retrieved the paper she sat on the couch and thumbed through the paper while waiting on the water to boil.

Rachel paused and thought about what had happened just a few hours ago. The conversation she had with James was interesting to say the least. His marriage was kind of funny the way he told it, but the part about giving his life to God was something that she was not expecting at all. She could see the passion in his eyes when he talked to her about God and getting her life together. Then she thought about the dream she just had. Could those events actually take place? I know that I have not done all that I should but, surely he will not send me to live in hell forever. As she pondered these things in her heart she began to recall the conversation with her friend at lunch the day before. The craziest thing though was that since speaking to Allana she has been hearing what appears to be a voice saying-I love you.

Just then the whistle on the kettle started to sound and it pulled her out of her thoughts. Putting the paper aside she rose from the couch and walked to the patio and opened the blinds. It was a beautiful morning. The sun was starting to rise and was giving off an array of colors to illuminate the skies. She opened the door and felt a warm breeze and decided to leave it open. Rachel headed to the kitchen to fix her tea and decided she might as well as eat breakfast. Surveying the fridge she opted for eggs, turkey sausage links and toast.

While preparing her breakfast, the events of yesterday started replaying in her mind once again. Not only did her best friend show up in town, tells her she is born again, whatever that mean, but so does her first true love. It was a conspiracy and she was not getting caught up in any of that. That stuff in her sleep, she thought, was just a dream. She went about preparing her meal. Once it was complete she decided to eat on the patio and watch the sun come up and read the paper. By this time it was eight o'clock. While enjoying her breakfast the telephone rang.

"Now who can that be this time of morning?" she asked herself while walking swiftly to catch the phone before it stopped ringing.

"Hello." Rachel said a little irritated.

"Good morning to you to." It was Allana.

"Hello Allana. What do I owe the honor of this call so early in the morning?" Rachel asked.

"I just finished praying and it was impressed upon me by God to call you. Did you have a peaceful rest?"

"It's funny that you ask me that. I was up until about one talking to James. We caught up on old times and he was telling me about how he came to accept Jesus as his personal Savior."

"Oh. So that was what he wanted to tell you?"

"And he talked about his marriage."

"I thought you said you did not see a ring."

"I didn't but he was married and now divorced. He says that he has never gotten over what we had."

"So does this mean you two are getting back together?"

"You know what? The answer is a definite no. He hurt me too bad and there is no way that I will forget that."

"But do you still love him?"

"Love? Allana, I have not seen James in about twenty years. I will always love him but, I am no longer in love with him. Besides, he is now Mr. Churchy and there is no way I am going to compete with that."

"You don't have to compete. Just surrender your life to Jesus and you both can move forward."

Rachel was beginning to get a little irritated. She felt her heart starting to race. As she took a deep breath she decided that today would not be the day for stress.

"Listen Allana, regardless of the past, James and I will always be friends. As far as romance is concerned, that is not going to happen. I do love him but as a friend loves another friend."

"Ok."

"What are you doing up so early? How did you know I would even be up?"

"In my prayer time God placed you on my heart. I know you did not sleep well. You have had dreams since we talked. Am I right?"

"Well, yes but how did you know? Besides, each time I had those dreams, which by the way, were utterly ridiculous, I had consumed a great amount of alcohol."

"What you need to know is that if God cannot get your attention while you are awake, He will speak to you while you are asleep. He wanted me to call you to talk to you and ask you one more time if you would like to attend church with me."

Rachel was listening to her friend. While listening to Allana, she could hear the words coming out of her mouth but all she heard over and over was---I love you. She was shaken and decided that she better do something. At least go hear what the preacher had to say.

"Alright Allana, I will go. What time is service and where is the church?"

"Amen. I'm glad you decided to come. The name of the church is the "The One Way to Christ Apostolic Church, located in Norcross. The service starts at eleven o'clock. Do you want me to come and get you?"

"No. I'll find it."

"Are you sure you are going to come?"

"Yes Allana I will be there. Now let me go finish my breakfast and I will see you later."

"Ok. Just remember to keep an open mind and heart. I love you my forever friend and I will see you soon."

"I love you too. See you soon."

Once Rachel hung up the phone she was in awe of what she had just committed herself to. She realized she had not been to church since the one time she attended while in college, and that was over fifteen years ago. Rachel went back to her finish eating her breakfast and reading the paper. She could not concentrate on the paper for trying to figure out what to wear to church.

On the other side of town Allana was giving God praise for doing what only He can do. She was thanking God for giving her a mind and heart to obey His voice. While getting dressed she had put her CD player on minimum blast due to the neighboring hotel guests. It was a mixed CD and the song playing at the time was "Lamb of God" by The New York Restoration Choir. As she began to get dressed she said a short prayer. 'Lord, thank you for being all that we need. Please let this be the day that my friend, your daughter Rachel gives her life to you. Please open her heart and spiritual eyes to see that those dreams are true and that everything that you showed her can and will come to pass. I thank you for your Divine, and perfect will to be done this day. In Jesus Name, Amen.' With that she went about dressing herself for what she knew would be a glorious time in the Lord.

James had risen early to get in his prayer time and bible reading. His mind would drift back to Rachel and the conversation they had the night before. At that moment the Lord had impressed upon him to pray and he did. 'Lord, I do not know what you are doing but I know what you want. What you want is for Rachel and others that don't know you to accept you as their Lord and Savior. I know that you do not want any to perish but to reign with you in eternity. I pray that all who attend a service today will be convicted in their heart and come confessing you and are baptized in your name and receive your Spirit. You did it for me and I know you will do it for them.

May the drug addict that come forth put their addiction for Meth, marijuana, cocaine and other mind altering drugs down and pick an

addiction to you and the love you have given
them through your death on the cross. Lord, the
prostitute who is selling his or her body for
money and looking for acceptance and
affirmation, take the blinders off so they can see
that you have already affirmed who they are.
Those that are confused by not knowing who
they are sexually because of the lie of the
enemy, let the truth of your word drop the scales
from their eyes to the unnaturalness of what is
perceived to be right. Bless the alcoholic to
come forth and put down the beer and wine
coolers and get buzzed on you and your word.
In the name of Jesus I thank you for all the souls
that are going to be claimed and reclaimed for
you all over this world for your kingdom.

Satan, the blood of Jesus is against you
and all that you stand for. Those that are bound

and entangled with all things not of God are loosed right now in the name of Jesus. Lord, everything happens for a reason and I thank you that even in the midst of our mess that you love us but are a gentleman and will never force yourself on us. Thank you for keeping us in our foolishness knowing that we would give the very essence of who we are over to you. Lord, I love you and thank you for being the King of kings and the Lord of lords. I thank you because you knew before the foundation of the world that I would be in this place, on this day and at this time. Because of who you are, I know that all things are working out for our good. You know the end from the beginning and even if we don't see it, I have faith to know that you do all things well. I thank you in advance for anointing the man or woman you have chosen to bring forth your word. Bless the choir as they set the tone for the services this day. In Jesus Name, Amen.'

James returned to getting dressed and started singing. He decided to call Rachel but had to call the front desk to get the connection. The phone rang, startling Rachel.

"Who is it this time she muttered to herself." She thought it was Allana calling to make sure she was still coming. Instead of saying hello she automatically said-

"Yes Allana, I'm getting dressed now." The person on the other end of the phone was not who she expected.

"Good morning Rachel. Did I catch you at a bad time? Sounds like you were half expecting someone else to be on the other end."

"Oh. Good morning James" Rachel said with a chuckle.

"Allana called and asked me to go to church with her and I decided to go. I'm getting dressed now. Is there something you needed?"

"No. You were on my mind and I thought I would call you and see how you were. So you're going to church. Where are you going?"

"Some church Allana is going to today. It's called One Way to Christ Apostolic Church in Norcross."

"Well good for you. I have heard of that church and they have a good time in the Lord over there. Can I call you later? Maybe we can get together for dinner. This time I promise to be on time."

"I'll have to see. I'm suppose to hang out with Allana today since she is leaving on Tuesday. By the way, how did you get this number?"

"Don't freak out. I called the front desk and they rang the number."

"I'm not freaking out. I just didn't remember giving it to you that's all."

"Well, I'm going to let you finish getting dressed. I will call you later about dinner."

"That will be fine. Like I said, I can't promise anything but you can call."

"You have a good time at church. And Rachel, remember that God loves you."

"Don't start that okay. I'm nervous enough about going."

"Why are you nervous? You've been to church before."

"I know, but not in about twenty years. Oh well, let me get this over with. I'll talk to you later."

"Ok. Goodbye."

After hanging up the telephone Rachel headed toward her bedroom to look for something to wear. The only things she had were the business suits that she wore to work and the evening dresses for the occasional club date. She settled on a sleek black dress with a jacket. Once Rachel decided on the outfit she gathered her accessories and the usual things that women wear. She hopped into the shower and noticed the heat from the water running down her neck and back was quite soothing. She realized she could not doddle but had to get ready because it was at least a 45 minute drive to the church.

After getting dressed and satisfied with her look she gathered her purse and keys and headed out the door. As she awaited the elevator she started getting nervous and almost changed her mind. If the elevator would not have opened just then she would have went back into her home. Maurice the doorman was working and as she entered the elevator they exchanged pleasantries. Once they reached their destination of the lobby she went to the door and requested her car from the valet. When her car arrived she got in and turned on the stereo system to listen to some music. Turning to a radio station she noticed that they were playing gospel music. Since she was already going to church she decided to put in an Herb Albert CD and listen to some jazz.

She pulled off and prepared for the drive to the church where Allana was going to be. It was a beautiful day with the sun high in the sky. Rachel reached up to retrieve her sunglasses from the holder in the area of the car lights. As she settled in for the ride her mind began to replay the dream that she had that night. Standing before God and being told to depart because her name was not listed in the book. Chills ran up her spine at the thought of not being in a place of peace for the rest of her life. But what she could not understand is why God would allow so much bad to happen to her. She could not wrap her head around losing her first love, her child, and being involved with a man that was using her and drugs.

There was no reason to go to church and believe in a God that would allow such things to happen. The conversations that she has had with the James and Allana have confounded her as to why now. 'There is no way that I will get sucked into the emotionalism of what happens at church', she thought to herself. As she continued to drive along she noticed the flow of traffic was picking up. She was driving the middle lane and decided to move to the far left so she would not miss her exit. After checking her mirrors, she proceeded to change lanes.

The praise team was singing and setting the tone of the services. As Allana was worshipping the Lord she began to pray for Rachel. 'Lord, I thank you for what you are going to do in this service because of who you are. Thank you for saving my friend Rachel. Break the barriers of her unbelief, doubt and fear. I pray that she will not be the same from this day forward. In Jesus Name, Amen.' Once she finished praying she joined back in the singing of the song at that moment, "The Blood That Jesus Shed".

Just as Rachel began to merge to the right, out of no where a semi-truck was barreling down and for whatever reason would not slow down. She swung in front of the semi just as the semi was changing to the middle lane. The semi truck clipped the rear of Rachel's car making her car spin out of control. Because the traffic was coming swiftly she barely had time to move her car out of the way of an oncoming vehicle. She over corrected and the front of the car hit the guardrail. When she hit the brakes they locked sending the car lunching forward. Her car flipped onto the roof as though someone had lifted the car from the rear and pushed it forward. The traffic in the far right lane had slowed to rubberneck, while the traffic in the middle and right lanes had slowed to a snails pace and at the scene had stopped. Several people had gotten out of their cars to assist as much as possible. Different ones had called for the police and paramedics. A couple of tall, strong and buff men had gone to the car to see if they could get her out.

When they had gotten to the car they were able to get a grip on what was left of the door and pull it away from the car. The two men worked together and in silence. They went about making sure her body was not receiving further damage and carefully removed her from the car. The men placed her on the ground away from the car just as it was beginning to give off a cloud of smoke. The impact was so severe that Rachel's face was bloody from the glass that was shattered into pieces. Both of her arms were broken as and her legs were disjointed and out of sorts. Her head had a gash that was spewing blood as well as an eye was dangling from the veins in its socket. These were just the injuries that could be seen. By the time they pulled her from the car the paramedics had showed up as well as the police. Just as quickly as they appeared they were gone.

James had decided to go to the church that Rachel was going to and made his way through the traffic that was backing up on the highway. When he was able to get to the far left lane, like everyone else he slowed to see what was going on. He had noticed the accident and said a prayer for the victim and all that were involved. The paramedics were busy attending to the victim and were amazed that she was still breathing. Barely, but she was still alive. Once they did what was necessary to get her ready they proceeded to transport her to Grace and Mercy Hospital which was a few miles off the next exit.

Because of the traffic James arrives at church just as the offering was being raised. As the congregation was walking around the altar placing their offering in the basket he noticed a familiar face. It was Allana, Rachel's best friend. He looked to see if he saw Rachel but to no avail. Once the offering was taken and the ones on the outside were allowed in, James made his way to where Allana was sitting. Allana looked up in surprise. As they exchanged hugs and pleasantries James looked around as if he were looking for someone.

"James. It has been a long time. How are you doing?"

"It has been a long time. I am doing fine. Rachel told me she was coming here today and I thought I would surprise her. Have you seen her?"

"No I haven't. I was going to go out in the hallway and call her cell. Maybe she got lost."

"Well, give it a few minutes. There was terrible accident on the highway on the way over. Maybe she got stuck in the traffic."

Just then the Psalmist had come to the microphone. The band was starting the introduction to one of Fred Hammond's song from his 'Pages of Life' CD. The song was "All Things Are Working" and the psalmist was really laying it down for the Lord. After the song started Allana went out to call Rachel.

The phone rang and rang. Finally the voicemail

picked up and Allana left a message. "Girl

where are you? The pastor will be up to speak

in a few minutes. Text me and let me know if

you r lost. See you soon." With that Allana

went back into the sanctuary and sat down.

"Did you reach her?"

"No. The voicemail picked up. I'm sure

she is on her way."

"Yeah, I know she was nervous when I

talked her this morning. Maybe she changed

her mind. Hopefully she didn't."

"I was shocked when I asked her and she

said yes. I did notice something strange in her

voice when I talked to her."

"Well, she'll be here soon. Hearing the Word is the best part of the service." James said with a grin.

Just then the song ended. The congregation was in euphoria with praises going to God for just being who He is. Bishop Ron McClurkin stepped to the podium and just stood there. He was not commanding silence but rather praising God himself. Then he spoke. "You may be wondering why I'm just standing here not saying anything. I'm just waiting to see what the Lord wants me to say. His presence is so thick that I don't want to speak out of turn. God is doing something for his people right now. In faith I want you to reach out and accept what He is doing."

The music reached a crescendo and the saints were shouting and praising God. If your spirit was in tune you could tell those who were dealing with the issues of life and giving God an 'in spite of praise'. Then there were the ones who had come through yet another test and giving God the greatest victory praise they could muster up. Just then the Pastor waved his hand toward the band to lower the volume because he had something to say. Once the music was lowered the pastor began to speak.

"Brothers and sisters God is here to heal you today. He not only wants to heal the physical body, but the spiritual body as well. The God that I serve, and the one you say you serve wants you to be whole in your mind. So many have been straddling the fence and do not have the peace of God. So many have believed the lies of the devil and that when it comes to the truth of God's word they only believe half or not sure if it is meant for them. God's word, my friends, is for everyone that believes and willing to receive. The bible says in Romans chapter 12 verse 2 says, 'And be not conformed to this world: but be ye transformed by the renewing of your mind, that ye may prove what is that good, and acceptable, and perfect will of God.' Now, as I see it, if your mind is not lined up with God's, which is his word, then you are out of order. The world tells you to be stressed out because of the different problems that may have arisen; being laid off from your job, being behind on your bills, can't make the mortgage payment.

We are not perfect. I have memory lapses as to not totally depending on God, but that does not excuse me from getting back in line with God and His word. There is no excuse for you either. God is moving in this place and if you want to receive from Him, the time is now. You can come to this altar right now and we will pray for you. If you want to stand in the gap for someone then you can do that too. God is no respecter of persons. The only thing he wants you to do is come in faith believing that he is a rewarder of them that diligently seek him."

The congregation began to move from their seats and toward the altar. James and Allana went forth and stood side by side. They looked at each other as if they knew what they were there for. They were not there for themselves but for their mutual friend Rachel who had not yet arrived. Once everyone had made their way to the altar the pastor began to speak again. "As a point of contact I want you to hold the hands of the person next to you.

Today is the day when things will begin to

change. No more mind games with the devil.

No more leaning on the

world for your help. No more stressing because

things are not the way you think they should be.

Like the song says which is also God's Word,

'For we know that all things work together for

good to them that love God, to them who are the

called according to his purpose'. Whatever it is

you or someone you know is going through,

God already knows the end from the beginning.

He is working it out.

Now let us pray. Father, in the name of

Jesus, we come to you right now to receive the

peace that you have for us. We put down the

stress. We put down the anxiety of not knowing

everything that you are doing. We pick up your

peace of mind because we will keep it on you. We pick up trust in you because we are going to acknowledge you in all our ways and you will lead us. Lord, I thank you for helping us to be more conscious of your presence in our lives. Thank you that we refuse to compromise with how the world says we ought to respond to the situations of life. In Jesus name we will live victoriously. Remind us that the only way to live according to your word and to be victorious in your word is to know what your word says.

Lord, help us to seek after the eternal things of God and not the temporary things. Help us not to be so quick to seek after stuff and things. But you said for us to—Seek first your kingdom and the things will be added to us. But also help us to remember that the things you add will not necessarily mean money and house and cars, but peace, happiness, and joy in the Holy Ghost. Lord, we especially pray for those who for one reason or another did not make it to church today. We ask that you watch over them and guide them into the light of your word. Keep them safe that they may accept you before it is everlasting too late. We thank you in advance for what you are doing and what you are going to do. In Jesus' mighty Name. Amen."

As the congregation made their way back to their seat James began to get a feeling like something was going on. He looked at Allana and gestured for the two of them to step into the foyer. Once they reached the entrance James began to speak.

"Allana, will you call Rachel again. I have an uneasy feeling and it's not going away."

"Sure. I'm sure she is okay. Like you said, she probably changed her mind and is at the mall."

The phone rang but this time it rang only once and automatically went to voicemail. Allana pulled the phone away from her ear and stared at James.

"What's wrong?" James asked.

"I'm not sure. The first time I called it rang several times then went to the voicemail. This time it went directly to voicemail on the first ring. You don't suppose she is in trouble do you?"

"Allana, I'm not so sure."

Just then her phone rang. She quickly answered it. On the other end was a voice she has not heard in a couple of months.

"Hello, Allana? This is Mary Abney, Rachel's mom. How are you?"

"I'm fine Mrs. Abney and you?"

"Well, I would be better if I could get a hold of Rachel. We have not spoken in a long while and I thought I would call just to say hi and check on her. I tried to call her but I can't reach her. I called your house and your husband told me where you were and that you had lunch with her yesterday."

"Yes Ma'am I did. I had invited her to church and she said she would be here. Actually I called this morning to make sure she was still coming and she said she was but she has not made it yet."

"I was watching the news and saw that there was a terrible car accident on the highway near her house. I just pray that she is not involved. When you talk to her will you please tell her to call me? Tell her that I love her."

"I sure will. You take care of yourself. I'm sure she will be here momentarily."

"You take care and call me when you get back home."

"I will Mrs. Abney."

As she hung up the phone she looked at James and had a look of confusion on her face. She just stared at James but not really seeing him.

"What's going on?"

"That was Rachel's mom. She wanted to talk to her but have not been able to get her on the phone. She said that she saw on the news about a terrible car accident and was concerned that Rachel may have been caught up in the mess."

"Well, there was an accident on the highway I took to get here. It is not far from where I'm staying which is in the same building as Rachel. I'm sure she is okay but we will wait until after service and go from there."

As they started to go back into the sanctuary, James received a Holy Ghost check in his spirit. It was the same feeling he had on the way out but only stronger. He stopped in his tracks and tilted his head slightly. Then he said,

"Allana, something is wrong with Rachel."

"What do you mean? How do you know?" Allana asked with a little alarm in her voice.

"The Lord just let me know. I don't know exactly what it is but I have to go."

"Let me get my things and I will go with you."

Allana went into the sanctuary to retrieve her things and then came back out. She looked at James and he was saying a prayer.

"Where are we going James?"

"That is what I was praying about. God said go to Grace and Mercy hospital."

"Are you sure?"

"He has never steered me wrong. Let's go."

They got to his car and pulled out of the parking lot. As they were driving he was letting the Lord lead him because he had no idea where he was going. Allana on the other hand was praying and looking on her phone for any news reports. She didn't find any but as they approached the highway going in the opposite direction she noticed the emergency vehicles just finishing the clean up. In about twenty minutes they were at the hospital. Once they parked they got out and walked swiftly into the emergency room to try to get some answers.

The emergency room was abuzz with activity. There were wall to wall patients and families waiting to be seen by a physician. James and Allana walked up to the nurse's station and started asking questions.

"Excuse me. I am looking for someone who may have been brought to this hospital." James began.

"Do you have a name?" the nurse asked.

"Her name is Rachel. Rachel Abney."

"Let me check and see. Wait here please."

When the nurse got up from her seat, she headed toward a set of double doors that was guarded by cop wannabes. She went through those doors and was gone for what seemed like forever but in actuality only about five minutes. When she returned she started talking and was interrupted by her supervisor.

"Sir, someone was brought in this morning but the person had not been identified. Are you family?"

"No." They both chimed in together.

"Well, unless you are family we cannot disclose any more information."

"You don't understand. All we want to know is if it is her or not. Her family lives in

Detroit. Can we at least see this person to possibly identify her?" Allana asked with agitation rising in her voice.

"Like I said, since you are not family you will not be able to go back there."

"Look, I am not trying to cause any problems. Our friend was suppose to meet us today and her mother has not been able to reach her. All we want to do is take a quick peek." James said.

"And again the answer is no. Rules are rules."

James was beginning to get upset. He turned away from Allana and the nurse and stared out of the windows that were adjacent to the entrance doors. By this time the nurse's supervisor had been called away to handle another matter. Allana walked up next to James and put her hand on his shoulder.

"Allana, I know she is here. I feel it in my spirit and know that God has directed us here."

"What are we going to do? They won't let us back there to see and verify that it is her."

"I am going to wait on God to see what he is going to do. I trust him that much and know that he won't let me down. For now we will just sit here and wait."

James and Allana found a couple of seats near the entrance of the double doors and made themselves comfortable. Two hours had passed, then four. Then a break came. One of the guards was passing and speaking to another. The conversation was nothing too specific until the passing officer asked had it been busy.

"Not too busy. There was real bad accident this morning on the highway. The car had been demolished. The craziest thing was that the driver of the car should be dead according to the EMT's but she is hanging on. But she is barely hanging on."

"Does the lady have any family?"

"Not that we know of. They located her purse and were trying to get a proper ID on her but things were scattered and burned in the fire of the car."

"Wow. I sure hope she makes it. Well, gotta keep making my rounds. I'll talk to you later."

"Alright. Have a good one."

After over hearing the conversation James walked up to the guard and decided to ask some questions.

"I couldn't help but over hear. That accident victim, how is she?"

"Mister, I'm not allowed to discuss patients' conditions. Are you family?"

"No sir. I am just a friend who thinks that the person you were discussing is my friend. She was brought here earlier but I am trying to get some answers."

"Well I don't have any for you." The guard said tersely. With that the guard walked away.

James went back and sat down next to Allana.

"James there has got to be a way for us to get back there without being too obvious that we don't know who we are looking for."

"I know. Listen, you stay here. I'm going for a walk. Take down my cell phone number. If anything transpires or you get any information before I get back I want you to call me."

"Where are you going?"

"I'm going to find a way around the system. I'll be back. You just pray."

"I will. Be careful."

With that James started walking and Allana started praying. James was thinking that there is always more than one way to get to any area of a hospital and if he took the right turns he would find his way behind the double doors from a different direction.

In the operating room the doctors were at a loss as to how she could have survived in the first place. There were several different surgeon specialists in the operating room. Dr. Wasserman, the head surgeon on duty, was amazed that the woman was still alive while trying to assess the full scope of damage. He addressed his team and was concerned with the bleeding that was coming from her head. A closer examination revealed there was a profusion of blood coming from the frontal lobe of the brain with a wound from the forehead to the middle of her head. Dr. Wasserman ordered a CT scan to determine the depth of the wound as well as to whether the bleeding was from a major artery.

Other team members were working on the limbs to try and put them back in place. Because Grace and Mercy hospital was a state of the art hospital, a patient could be fully assessed without leaving the area. It was because of this the doctor decided to do a full body scan and MRI to further determine the internal damage of the patient. With this information the doctor could make a decision as to what was the most crucial injury to work on first to save her life. When the first of the test began to unfold it was a cause for great concern.

The patient's brain was bleeding from an artery that would need to be repaired. This type of injury left ninety percent of the patients dead. In order to do the repair work they would have to move expeditiously if she was to have any chance of living. Her quality of life may not be what it was but she was alive, which was a miracle in itself. Once the full scan was complete, the injuries were great. In the accident she had damage to her spleen which would have to be removed, as well as a laceration on her liver, bruised kidney and a punctured lung. Both of her legs were broken and disjointed as well as both arms.

After the assessment was done preparation was made for surgery to stop the bleeding in her brain as well as repair the lung. Because these were the most damaging injuries, everything else was put on hold until a later time.

"A team will be trying to stop the bleeding in her brain and another team will be working on the puncture in her lungs. This patient is in for a long road of recovery and I don't want any mistakes. Scrub up and meet me back here in ten minutes. Nurses, you know what to do. Check the blood supply and make sure we have plenty on hand. Now let's get moving because time is of the essence." Everyone scrambled to prepare to do their part in trying to save this woman's life.

As James made his way through the hospital hallways, he noticed the scurrying of a cluster of doctors. He didn't say anything but just lingered back and listened.

"That poor woman, I can't believe she is still alive." One nurse said as she passed.

"I know. I bet her family is worried sick. I heard it was a freak accident on the highway this morning." The other nurse had said.

This was the break James needed. He followed the nurses as far as he could before he was stopped with a door that said "NO ENTRANCE" and a plate where a security pass had to be swiped to enter. Once he saw the sign he hovered around a water fountain hoping to slide in as doctors or nurses went through the doors. Sure enough a couple of minutes later a few doctors used their pass to get through the doors. He looked in as they went and saw them go a few feet then turn into a room. He wanted to see if there was a place to duck into if someone spotted him once he got past the doors. He noticed to the right of the room a row of curtains with beds behind them that were empty.

A few minutes later a few nurses came up and swiped their card. He figured it's now or never. Once they were through the door, he waited until the last possible moment and then slid in. After he made sure he was not seen he walked with stealth like precision without drawing attention to himself. James was able to get as close as possible without being seen and was able to peek in through a square window that was on the entrance of the door where everyone was. There were doctors and nurses all over the place and he could not see the patient. Then all of a sudden the doctor moved and he saw her. It was Rachel.

At that moment James felt his stomach make a u-turn. He felt a noise coming up and he quickly covered his mouth as not to draw attention to himself. Tears were burning the rims of his eyes as he tried to see all he could see. Once he saw all that he could stand he turned and left as quickly as he came. After getting back to the safety zone of where he was allowed to be James broke down and started to cry. He took out his phone and called Allana. She quickly picked up the phone.

"Hello."

"Allana, it's her. It's Rachel and she looks bad."

"James, are you sure?"

"Yes I'm sure. I would know her anywhere, even in the state she is in now." James said.

"Now what do we do?"

"First we pray. Then we talk to the powers that be of the hospital. Once we talk to them we call her parents. I'm on my way back around there. Ask them where the chapel is and we will go there."

"Ok."

Allana hung up the phone and sat in her seat. She was numb and could not move. She thought about Rachel's mother and the rest of her family. She went to the guard and asked him for directions to the chapel. Once she received the information she sat back down to wait for James. Just then a police officer came to the guard station and gave some information about the patient that was brought in earlier.

"We ran the plates of the woman they brought in earlier. Her name is Rachel Abney. We have some of her belongings that were recovered from the scene." The officer said.

"I will see to it that we get them to the right person". The guard said.

Allana went to the guard station and spoke up.

"Excuse me. I couldn't help but over hear you give the name of the person in that accident. She is my best friend. May I take charge of her things?"

The police officer spoke up before the guard had a chance to be rude yet again.

"Miss?"

"Mrs. Forest."

"Well Mrs. Forest, it is not our policy to hand over personal property to anyone without family permission."

"Officer, she has no family here in town. I am her best friend visiting from out of town. Look, I have not called her mother yet because I wanted to be sure it was her before I upset her unnecessarily."

"I really don't know what to tell you."

"Listen, I'm going to have to call her eventually. If I dialed the number would you talk her and ask her if it would be okay to accept her things and be the spokes person until someone gets here from out of town?"

The guard spoke up and said, "I doubt if the officer has time to be a go between. He has work to do."

Allana glared at the police wannabe and said a silent prayer before speaking.

"Oh that's ok. Go ahead and make the call and I will do the talking." The officer said. Allana dialed the number and gave the phone to the officer. She looked at the guard who was fuming right about now. He looked at her and started to say something but she spoke first. "Favor ain't fair."

She heard the officer start to speak to Rachel's mother just as James walked up.

"Hello. Yes, this is Officer Gerald Seats. Do you have a daughter by the name of Rachel Abney?"

"Yes. My God what has happened to her?"

"Well Ma'am there has been an accident and your daughter is here at Grace and Mercy hospital in Atlanta. There is someone her by the name of Mrs. Allana Forest who wishes to take possession of her things."

"Is my daughter dead?"

"All I know is that she is in the operating room. She was pretty bad off when she was brought in but I have not heard anything else." As she was whimpering she spoke again.

"Allana is my daughter's best friend. Is there a doctor or someone I can speak to in order to stay informed until I get there?"

"Yes Ma'am. I will get the head nurse on duty and you can speak to her. I'm sorry for your trouble and I pray that your daughter will be well."

"Thank you officer Seats." Mrs. Abney said.

"I'm going to take your phone to the head nurse. Follow me and we will get you to your friend."

"This is also a childhood friend. Can he come also?"

"Sure."

Allana and James followed the officer past the guard and she wanted to stick her tongue out at him but decided to remain mature about the situation.

"Nurse Pouty, please assist these people. They are with the young lady that was brought in about an hour ago. Her mother is on the phone and wishes to speak to you."

"Thank you Officer Seats. Hello, this is nurse Pouty."

"Yes ma'am, I will be more than glad to allow them full access to your daughter until you are able to be here. No problem."

With that the nurse handed the phone to Allana and she took it and spoke to Mrs. Abney.

"Yes Mrs. Abney. I know it is hard, but she will be okay. You don't understand. I have not spoken to her in months. We had lunch yesterday and had a misunderstanding. I don't know what I will do if she is taken from me before she's had a chance to make things right. Mrs. Abney, God is watching over her and we are just going to pray that God's divine will be done. I was due to leave and go home on Tuesday but I will not leave until you are here and know that she is going to be all right."

"I'll be there as soon as I can arrange a flight. I'll call you when I get in. Thank you Allana."

"You don't have thank me. She would do the same for me. That's what friends are for. James is here with me also."

"James? You mean James Rivers? What is he doing there?"

"It's a long story. I will have him pick you up at the airport and you can talk from there."

"Ok baby. Thanks again, here. I'll be there as soon as I can."

"Ok."

With that they hung up. She turned and looked at James and saw the tears in his eyes and she began to cry. They hugged and Allana spoke to the nurse.

"Do we need a pass to get in and out of here?"

"Yes. Go to the registration desk and get a sticker and have them put the patients name on it and you will be able to come and go as you wish."

"Thank you. We are going to the chapel and we will return shortly. Here is my cell number. If there is any word, please call me."

"I will." Nurse Pouty said.

They went to the registration desk to retrieve their name tags and Allana lead James to the chapel. As James and Allana reached the chapel another family was coming out. They noticed the family was teary eyed and had the look of worry and concern on their face. James opened the door for Allana and followed her into the room where they noticed another family was there. The room was silent as everyone was in their own personal space in their hearts and minds. They took a seat and at first just sat there looking at the hand carved image of Jesus on the cross at the altar in the front of the room.

Allana spoke first. "James, this can't be happening. I just saw her yesterday at lunch."

"I saw her last night. We got caught up on the events of our lives. When I left she was kind of miffed at me but we were good."

"She was a little upset with me too. I was telling her how I came to accept Jesus as my Lord and Savior. Boy was she upset."

"That was the same reason she was mad at me. Could it be that she saw something in us that she wanted and was to proud to admit it?"

"I don't know. I had asked her to come to church with me but she said no. When I called her back this morning she had changed her mind. I was so looking forward to seeing what God was going to do for her today."

"I know. That is why I decided to join you all. Plus I wanted to hear this great man of God I have been hearing about."

"As I look at that cross in the front of the room, I can't help but think that God is up to something."

"Why do you say that?"

"Well, I have only been saved a short time myself, but I know that God does not deal in coincidences. Everything happens for a reason."

"I see your point."

Just then the other family made nice and departed the chapel. Their countenance was different from the first family. They had a look of peace. Then like a light bulb that had gone off in his head he said.

"You know what? God is control of this situation. We may be concerned for Rachel's welfare but he is concerned with her soul. I believe that even in the state that she is in he is ministering to her right now."

"I wonder what happened that made her change her mind."

"Only God knows the answer to that question. The only thing we need to do right now is pray, trust and believe that God's divine will be done."

"You're right."

Just then James led them both in prayer.

"Father, it is in the name of Jesus that we are here on behalf of your child Rachel. Lord, we know that all things work together for the good of them that love you and are the called according to your purpose. Lord, please be with Rachel at this time. Guide the surgeons hand as they do what you have given them the knowledge and skill to do. She is fearfully and wonderfully made in your image. We thank you for being wounded for our transgression and bruised for our iniquities. We thank you for the chastisement of our peace being upon you. We thank you for by every stripe that you endured we are healed. Lord, the outside body is flesh and can be healed of the bruises and bumps, but Lord, it is more important that the soul be healed. If her soul is healed, then no matter what, she will be forever with you in paradise.

It is because of you that we are able to stand in complete faith of your goodness and grace. It is because of you and what you did on

Calvary that we are able to petition to you this day for grace and mercy. Thank you in advance for what you are doing and going to do for Rachel and her family. We give a right now and in spite of praise. What we see is not what is because of who you are. Hallelujah. Your name, Father, is above every name. We give you glory, honor and praise, in Jesus' Name. Amen."

Once James finished praying they started to give God some praise. Allana was already pacing back and forth while speaking in her heavenly language with James following suit. The glory of the Lord was so heavy in the room that everyone that came in was slain in the spirit and fell where they sat or stood. While James was worshipping and praising the Lord, he got a check in his spirit and started laying hands on those that had come in. There was no resistance for when God is in the building sin sick souls are healed. He went to each one individually and

through him God ministered to everyone, which was about ten people. After he finished he sat down and just lingered in the presence of the Lord. Allana was still worshipping God as she took a seat next to James. One by one as the individuals regain their composure they started to leave and as they did they shook James' hand and said thank you. All he could do was nod his head in humbleness knowing that it was not him but the all powerful God that showed up and did what He does best, touch the hearts of his people. Just then Allana's phone rang and it was Rachel's mom.

"Hello Mrs. Abney."

"I just wanted to let you know that I will arrive at ten fifteen. It's a non-stop flight."

"That will be fine. James or I will be there to pick you up. You are welcome to stay with me at my hotel."

"I appreciate that, but I doubt if I will be leaving the hospital until I find out how my baby is doing."

"I understand. The offer stands. We will be at the airport to pick you up. Will Mr. Abney be with you?"

"He will be out tomorrow. He has to make sure the house is secure since the kids are no longer in close proximity. Have you heard anything more about Rachel?"

Allana hesitated because she did not want to alarm her with the information that James had given her.

"No Ma'am. She is still in surgery."

"Prayerfully she will be out by the time I get there. I will see you soon."

"Ok."

Allana hung up the phone and clutched it to her chest and hung her head.

"I pray that her mother is strong enough to handle what is surely a frightening sight of her daughter."

"I'm sure she can handle it. I remember her as a strong woman of faith when we were growing up."

Just then the nurse, Ms. Pouty came through the door.

"Nurse Pouty, has there been any word as to the condition of our friend?"

"No not yet. The injuries were quite extensive so it may be while. Why don't go to the cafeteria and get something to eat or drink. If something comes up we have the cell phone number."

James looked at his watch and saw that it was already four o'clock. He decided that although he was hungry he would abstain from food until he knows Rachel will be alright.
"I'm going to get a bottle of water, do you want anything?" he asked Allana.
Allana had realized that she had not eaten since before leaving for church. She too decided to abstain from food until she found out about her friend. Neither one knew what the others plans were.

"I'll take some water as well."

"Ok. I'll be right back." James replied.
Meanwhile, the operating room where Rachel
was being taken care of was a buzz with
activity.

"There is hemorrhaging in the brain.
We have to stop this bleeding or she will die."
Dr. Wasserman stated rather emphatically.
There was another doctor, Dr. Justin
Smitherithers, who was working on the
punctured lungs.

"I know there is a lot of internal
bleeding here as well. This woman is in such
awful shape, but we must keep going." was his
reply.
The technician who was monitoring her vitals
interrupted the doctors.

"Dr.'s, her heart rate is slowing down at a tremendous rate. We are losing her."

Trying to increase the activity in her heart was becoming a challenge because of the severity of Rachel's injuries. Dr. Smitherithers began moving as quickly as possible. There were only a few more stitches that needed to be made on the lungs and then he would be finished. In the meantime he asked Dr. Stein to massage the heart until he was able to assist.

"Maybe there is a way to actually shut her down until we can get the hemorrhage in her head to stop. Dr. Wasserman said.

"But if we shut her down completely, she could die. The injuries she has sustained will not allow such a procedure." Dr. Stein replied.

"If we don't do something she is going to die anyway."

Just then while the doctors were trying to decide what to do the bleeding in her head stopped. There was still swelling but the bleeding had stopped.

"Her blood pressure had come back up and her breathing rate is sluggish but steady." The technician announced.

The doctors looked at each other. "What just happened?" Dr. Wasserman asked.

"I don't know but let's close up the head wound and you finish the work on the lungs. We will have to work on the liver and kidneys at another time. For now, looking at the liver it is ok to say that medication will be able to keep them functioning until we can return to repair them. With the right combination of medication the liver can repair itself."

"What about her kidneys?" Dr. Smitherithers asked.

"We will monitor her kidneys and if necessary we will repair them. For now let's move forward with making sure the lungs and hemorrhaging has been successfully stopped. As for her arms and legs, we will set them for now, but in order for them to heal properly they will have to be broken and reset."

As the doctors began their procedure of closing her up, Rachel flat lined.

James looked at his watch. It was seven-thirty in the evening.

"I wish somebody would come out and tell us what is going on."

"I know. I'm sure she's fine though. It just takes time to do what needs to be done." With that James spoke up. "I'm going to go pick up Mrs. Abney. By the time I get to the airport the plane will have landed and she should be going through baggage claims to gather her luggage. I'll be back as soon as I can."

Allana looked at her watch. "I didn't know it was this late. You go ahead. If anything happens I will call you on your cell phone."

James stood up and started to leave. He stopped and just stood there for a brief moment. He lowered his head and closed his eyes. Allana looked at him and asked, "What's wrong?"

"Something is going on. I'm not sure what but it's not good. I'm going to go. You make sure you call if you hear anything, you understand?"

"Yeah, sure James I will. You know I will."

James started walking swiftly toward his car. "Lord, I don't know what is going on but I trust you." He got into his car and left to pick up Rachel's mother.

Back in the operating room the doctors, nurses and technicians are scrambling to try and resuscitate Rachel who heart has stopped. While this was taking place Rachel's spirit was hovering over the operating room. Rachel was looking down and seeing the doctors working on her and was horrified at what she is seeing. She was saying to herself, "What's going on? I was on my way to church and now I'm in this place and it appears I have died." She tried to speak to let the people know that she was alive and was ok but they couldn't hear her.

Just then she was standing in the presence of a large white throne. She vaguely remembers being in this place but not sure. Then she heard a voice speak. The voice sounded like rushing water. It was strong and authoritative but loving.

"Rachel, I have loved you from the foundation of the world. I sent my Son to die and shed His blood for you, but you rejected me as you grew older."

Rachel, not understanding why, was bowed down before Him. She started crying and said, "I do believe in you. I was just so angry because everybody that I trusted ended up hurting me in one way or another."

"What you fail to realize is that I always work things out for your good. Everything you have gone through to this point was for the express purpose of drawing you closer to me. But because you had grown selfish, you thought that I was not with you. I have never left or forsaken you."

"I'm so sorry."

He reached down and caressed her head. Then Rachel lifted her head to look into his face but the glory was so blinding that she could not behold his face but for a split second.

"Why do I have to die now? Please give me another chance to get right. You saw that I was on my way to church when this happened. Can I go back?"

The doctors were using the defibrillator to revive her. No matter what they did nothing seemed to work. They worked on her for more than an hour. Then the doctors decided to call her death.

"There is nothing else we can do. The time is ten fifteen." Dr. Wasserman said. Everyone just stopped what they were doing and the room was totally silent for what seemed to be forever.

"Someone needs to talk to the family." Dr. Stein had said somberly.

"I understand there is no family, but I will check with the nurse." Dr. Wasserman said.

Once Dr. Wasserman checked with the nurse and found there were people awaiting word he walked to the waiting room to perform the daunting task of giving the news. Allana looked up and saw the doctor and stood up.

"Doctor, how did it go? How is Rachel doing?" She asked.

The look on the doctor's face told the story.

"Mrs. Forest, I regret to inform you that she did not make it. Her injuries were so extensive. I don't know what happened. It was touch and go but we were able to get her stable enough with the most life threatening injuries to keep her alive with the hopes of dealing with the other things at a later time."

"Can I see her?" Allana asked as tears started streaming down her face.

"I don't think that would be a good idea. We are waiting for morgue to pick her up."

"No. You have to wait. Her mother is on her way here from the airport and she is going to want to see her. Please doctor, she has not seen her or talked to her daughter in months."

"What I will do is ask the nurses to clean up as much of the blood on her as possible. Once her mother arrive let us know and we will talk to her and take her back to see her. Will that be alright?"

"Yes that will be fine."

The doctor looked at Allana and said, "I am really sorry for your loss." And then he walked away. Allana looked at him and nodded her head. She opened her phone and dialed James' number. He answered on the first ring.

"Hello."

"James, have you picked up Mrs. Abney?"

"Yes. She's sitting next to me. What's going on?"

"No. Don't say it."

"Yes. She's gone. The doctor just came out and told me."

James started to cry and Mrs. Abney knew something was wrong. He looked at her and shook his head. Mrs. Abney reached for the phone and spoke to Allana.

"Allana, how is my baby doing?" In her gut she already knew.

"Mrs. Abney, I am really sorry but she is gone. She did not make it through surgery."

"We will be there shortly."

"Mrs. Abney, they are going to wait for you to see her before they take her away."

"That will be nice. I want you to pull yourself together. Everything will be alright."

"Yes Ma'am."

James was crying so uncontrollably that he had to pull to the side of the road. All he could do was put the car in park and lean on the steering wheel. Mrs. Abney began to cry heavy sobs as well.

"My baby girl, I am so sorry the last words we spoke were in an argument. Lord, please forgive me." They hugged each other and then James spoke and said,

"I have and always will love Rachel. I'm sorry she did not accept Christ before now."

Once they gathered themselves, James put the car back in drive and merged into the traffic and continued on to the hospital. They reached the parking lot of the hospital in about twenty minuets. After putting the car in park, he got out and went around and helped Mrs.

Abney out of the car. They walked swiftly into the waiting room where Allana had met them at the door. She embraced Mrs. Abney and they started crying once again. Then James joined in on the hugging. After this they went to the nurse station and asked for the doctor in charge. The nurse quickly obliged her and left to find Dr. Wasserman. The wait was unbearable but it was not long when Allana noticed the doctor and started walking toward him with James and Mrs. Abney.

"Dr. Wasserman, this is Rachel's mother Mrs. Abney."
He extended his hand to shake Mrs. Abney's and James' hand.

"Doctor, what happened?" Mrs. Abney asked.

"Mrs. Abney, her injuries were quite extensive. We had to ascertain which injuries were the most life threatening. After discovering the bleeding on her brain and the punctured lung, we, the other doctors and I, decided to deal with those two areas first and foremost. The injuries to her kidneys, liver and spleen were serious, but they were not life threatening."

"So doctor, what caused her death?" James asked.

"That is what is troubling. It was touch and go for a brief time. The bleeding on her brain had stopped and Dr. Smitherithers had finished repairing her lungs. We stitched her and closed up the wounds. Her vitals were such that they did indicate a problem. Out of nowhere she flat lined. We tried to revive her for little more than an hour."

"Can I see my daughter now? I can make the formal identification of who she is but I need to say good-bye to my daughter."

"Yes Ma'am. Follow me."

Mrs. Abney and Allana followed the doctor but James hung back.

"James, are you coming?" Allana asked.

"I'll be there in a minute." He replied.

James was in his own thoughts and did not want to see Rachel just yet. He sat down in a seat near the windows and just stared out into the darkness. 'Lord, is that what that check in my spirit was about earlier? Were you preparing me for this very moment? I know to be absent from the body is to be in your presence but she will not be with you because she had not given her life to you. I don't understand but I trust you. It is hard enough accepting the death of a loved one that has given their life to you. Just give Mrs. Abney the strength she needs to deal with this.'

James arose and walked toward the operating room where Mrs. Abney, Allana and the doctor were viewing Rachel's body. He walked slowly into the room and put his arms around both women and just looked at her. The nurses cleaned off as much blood as they could to make her presentable before her family and friends came to see her. Mrs. Abney was caressing her daughter's hand as tears were streaming down her cheeks like a slow but steady waterfall. Allana had leaned her head on James shoulder and was just staring at her friend. James looked at his watch and noticed that it was eleven forty-five. He was silent and then he got another check in his spirit.

"Mrs. Abney and Allana may I be alone with Rachel?"

Mrs. Abney looked up at James as did Allana. They were curious but they obliged him.

"Come on Allana, James needs a private moment with Rachel. Doctor, will that be alright?"

"Yes, that will be fine."

With that they all left the room. James pulled up a stool and sat down and just stared at Rachel. "My lovely Rachel, you will never know how much I really love you." He took Rachel's hand and bowed his head and started to pray silently. "Lord, you said in your Word that when we have your Spirit we shall do great things for your glory. We would be able to take up serpents, drink any deadly thing and it will not harm us and lay hands on the sick and they shall recover. If it be your will for me to be used of you please allow Rachel to be raised from death. Cause her to be raised from this natural death that will cause her to spend eternity in hell."

James stopped talking and was listening for the Lord to speak. He was so overcome from emotion that he started crying. Then he stood up, walked around the table where Rachel was laying. When he walked back around he stopped at the foot of the bed and stepped back. He stretched out his hand over her without touching her and with a bold, confident voice he said, "Death, in the Name of Jesus, loose her and let her go." James did not move a muscle and just watched.

While all of this was going on, Mrs. Abney, Allana, and the doctor was looking through the square glass window. Suddenly Rachel's body jerked ever so slightly. The three observers gasped as they saw what looked like movement. Though the doctor saw what the other two saw he said, "It's just rigor mortis setting in." But what the doctor was really thinking was that the body has not had enough time to start that process yet.

In another strong voice James said, "In the name of Jesus, physical body be healed. In the name of Jesus, Spiritual body, be healed. From this day forward you have been spiritually and physically made whole, in Jesus Name."

Again he did not move a muscle. Then he saw the transformation starting to take place. Every where there was a scar, they started to heal over. Her legs and arms which were disjointed due to breakage started lining up and popping back into place. Those internal injuries that can not be seen were being put back together. Rachel's kidneys, spleen, liver and lungs were being healed back to normal. The swelling in her head was going down.

While all of this was going on the observers were crying. The doctor was without words for he has never seen such a miracle in his entire life of being a physician and surgeon. He was standing in awe with his hand over his mouth.

"Rachel, in the name of Jesus open your eyes." James said.

With that command Rachel's eyes fluttered a few times and then finally opened. James began to praise God. He then waved for

Mrs. Abney, Allana, and the Doctor to come into the room. Because they could not hear what James was saying they were able to see it for themselves. The three stopped in their tracks when what they saw was nothing of what they remembered. Every wound was no where to be seen. On top of that her eyes were open. They moved closer and the doctor began to examine her. He used his stethoscope and checked her heart, breathing and bowels through her stomach. He used his pen light to look into her eyes. They reacted to the light and were normal. He moved his hands up and down each leg and arm. All bones were back in place.

"Will you excuse me for just a moment please?" With that he left the room and went to get Dr.'s Stein and Smitherithers. When they returned the two doctors were just as stunned as Dr. Wasserman.

"What is going on here? I thought we pronounced her dead." Dr. Stein said.

In unison Dr. Wasserman and Dr. Smitherithers said, "We did."

While James, Mrs. Abney, and Allana huddled together the other two doctors did what Dr. Wasserman did and examined her from head to toe. Once they concluded their examination of the visible outer body, they conducted an MRI and CT scan on the inside to see it for themselves. It was then that friends and mother left the room.

"James, what happened in there? I mean, I see what happened, but what happened?"

"God is what happened. All I did was what God told me to do. I was praying and trying to get closure, but I was concerned for her eternal soul."

"We saw you walking around the table. What was that all about?" Mrs. Abney asked.

"Well, as God was speaking I was making sure it was him and not me being emotional. I never want to get in the way of God doing whatever he wants to do. It had no significance other than me trying to get out of the way."

Just then the doctors came out of the room with tears in their eyes.

"This is remarkable. I was there when they brought her in and we knew it would be a slim chance at best that she would live. And if she did live she would have a long road back in recovery."

"Every organ, bone structure and brain function is back to normal. We want to keep her here for observation and run more test to ensure that everything is right before we discharge her." The other doctor said.

"We declared her dead at ten fifteen. It is now midnight that we say without hesitation she is alive."

"When God does something, it is done well and completely" Mrs. Abney said. Everyone nodded in agreement. Word spread quickly throughout the hospital of what has transpired. The doctors went to their office while James, Mrs. Abney, and Allana went back into the operating room to be with Rachel. She was laying there with her eyes still open but tears running down the sides of her face. Her mother brushed her hair back and kissed her on the forehead. "Mommy is here." They made eye contact and spoke volumes without opening their mouths to utter one word. Allana stepped up on the other side and gave her friend and peck on the cheek and said, "I love you gurlie."

James took Allana's hand and reached across and took Mrs. Abney's hand while they held Rachel's.

"Lord, we thank you for what you have done this night. Like Paul and Silas, it was at midnight that they began to sing praises unto you. Thank you for giving us back Rachel. We don't know what you are going to do from here but we thank you in advance and give you the glory. You are the Alpha and Omega, the beginning and the end. You knew from the foundations of the world that we were going to be in this place, at this time.

Thank you for allowing us to be a part of your miraculous power of healing. Not only the healing of the body but of the soul. This hospital will never be the same because of you. Lives will never be the same because of you. We are humbled to be in your presence and we bow our hearts to you. As we move forward from this place help us to always remember that if we take you out of the box miracles can and do take place. It is with gratitude and humility that we say Thank You Jesus. In Jesus Name, Amen."

Rachel began to move her mouth like she was trying to say something but the words were not coming out. Mrs. Abney leaned in to try to hear her daughter. When she got close enough she heard her daughter say with a raspy voice, "I died didn't I?"

Mrs. Abney looked around at James and Allana. When she looked back at Rachel she nodded her head yes. Then tears started to stream down her face.

"But you are back with us Rachel." Allana spoke up and said.

James moved in so Rachel could see him more clearly.

"God has done a wonderful thing and allowed you to come back to us. We can talk about it more at a later time. They are going to keep you here a couple of days to run some test and then they will send you home. We are not going anywhere." James said with a broad grin on his face.

Straining to talk, Rachel just whispered, "Ok."

In her heart Rachel knew exactly what had happened. She lay there just thinking of what had taken place and wanted to tell everyone but since she was having a hard time talking she thought she would just wait for when the time was right. She was really glad that her mother was there. The nurses came in to finish cleaning her up so James, Allana and Mrs. Abney left the room. The nurses went about doing their jobs and commenting to Rachel how they were glad that everything turned out the way it did. They were very gentle and kind while moving her around to clean her up. Finally they were done and were getting ready to leave when Rachel strained to reach out to them. She was able to tap one of the nurses and motion her finger to lean in so she could say something to her.

"Yes Ma'am?"

"God bless you." She whispered.

The nurses looked at her and smiled warmly and then left the room. Her fan club came back in and had gathered around her bed when an orderly came in to transport her to her hospital room. They followed them to another area of the hospital and it was there that they helped Rachel get comfortable. As the news of Rachel's death and then being alive again an hour or so after being declared dead spread, someone has called the news media. The accident was already the top story on the evening news but now there was a media frenzy building in the waiting room of the emergency area and outside of the hospital causing traffic to back up for those trying to get in to receive services.

"This is Kelly Bryant of WATL TV and we are here at Grace and Mercy Hospital where an alleged miracle has taken place. As we reported earlier, there was a serious accident on the highway where a car was clipped on the rear fender by a semi trailer truck while changing lanes causing the accident. The semi kept going, but the car has been totaled. We were told by an unnamed source, the victim, Rachel Abney, when brought in was barely breathing and the doctors worked on her non stop for several hours.

According to our source, she was declared dead at around ten fifteen but was declared alive again at twelve fifteen, two hours later. We are waiting on a statement from the doctors who worked on her in the operating room. We will keep you updated as this story progresses. This is Kelly Bryant, live at Grace and Mercy Hospital. We now return you back to your regular programming."

Rachel and her family were unaware of what was going on outside while she was getting settled into her room. Because it was a private room, they were able to have another bed wheeled in so her mother, Mrs. Abney, could stay with her daughter. Rachel was a little restless but tired and kept drifting in and out of sleep. She finally settled down enough to get comfortable and drifted off into a deep sleep. Mrs. Abney asked James to retrieve her bags from the car so she too could get comfortable. As James was leaving the room, Allana stopped him.

"James, wait up."

"What's wrong Allana?"

"Oh nothing. I'm just still dumbfounded as to what has happened here tonight."

"I know. God sure is good."

"I know. What I don't understand is why? I have never heard of anything like this happening except in the bible days."

"Well, God still heals and he still raises people from the dead, not only spiritually but naturally. God will use whoever wants to be used by him. If our hearts and mind are open to hear from him then when he speaks we will follow."

"But why are there are people who don't believe that the Old Testament is not relevant if they believe in God? God does and speaking in tongues is for us today also according to Acts 2:39. They insist on labeling us as a cult. "

"I know. The fact is that they are speaking out of ignorance and lack of faith. What they can't understand with their finite minds or explain with intellectuality they say it is not true or is not for today."

"That makes sense. So what you are saying is that in order to know God and to trust Him above all in spite of everything else we must take him out of the box."

"That's right. If you think he can do only certain things, then that is all he will do for you. But don't limit my faith and understanding of who he is just because you are limited in your faith and understanding. We can always learn from God's word from Genesis to Revelation. It is all relevant."

"I see. Just like they say 'If you don't know where you've been then you don't know where you're going.' It's true with God's word then?"

"Actually it is. The Old Testament is the New Testament contained, and the New Testament is the Old Testament explained. Even though we are under grace, the whole bible is relevant and we can learn from the old as well as the new."

"Thank you for helping me with that. Like I said, I have only been saved a short time but I want all the understanding that God has for me."

"No problem. I'm going to go get Mrs. Abney's things. Can I get you anything?"

"No thanks."

"Ok. I'll be right back."

Just as James descended from the elevator on the first floor he noticed a crowd of people and was wondering what was going on. The closer he got to the door to go to the car he noticed the different news crews and the crowd that had gathered. Then he heard someone say, "That guy right there was with the miracle lady." Everyone turned around and looked at him and started bombarding him with questions. When James looked around he noticed that it was the guard that had given them a hard time earlier that made it known who he was.

"Are you the husband of the lady that was brought in earlier?" One reporter asked. Before he had a chance to answer, someone asked,

"Did you see what happened in the operating room? What do you make of it?"

James stopped and the only thing that he knew he was suppose say at this time was, "No comment."

The reporters kept after him as he turned and started toward the car. Because they followed him he got in the car and decided to act like he was leaving. He decided that he would try to find an out of the parking space and walk back to the hospital but go through another entrance. Once he pulled off, the crowd that followed him turned around and started walking back toward the hospital entrance. James circled the block and found a parking space about a block away. He got out and walked toward another entrance and was able to enter without being seen. He went up to the sixth floor and headed toward Rachel's room but stopped at the nurse's station first.

"I would like to speak to someone in charge."

"Yes sir. One moment please." One of the nurses said.

"I'm head nurse Turner, how can I help you?"

"I wish to ask you not to allow anyone in to see Rachel Abney unless they have clearance from either me or her mother. There are reporters sniffing around and this has been a very rough day for all involved."

"I have heard about Ms. Abney and understand. Are you her husband?" Nurse Turner had asked.

"Well no just a childhood friend."

"Unfortunately I can only honor that request if it came from her mother."

"I understand. I will talk to her and I am sure she will get back with you. Thank you."

"You are welcome. Can I help you with anything else?"

"No that will be all."

James started toward Rachel's room, which was at the end of the hall. As he entered, he noticed Mrs. Abney sitting next to her daughter, holding her hand and stroking her forehead with the other hand. Allana was staring out of the window so deep in thought that she did not hear him come in. He put Mrs. Abney's bags down and walked over to Allana and tapped her on the shoulder. She jumped ever so slightly and turned toward James and grinned a little but noticed she had a tear coming down her face.

"What's wrong?"

"I was just going over the events of the day and evening and how I am humbled to have been able to witness for myself the power of God."

"Yeah, it's amazing. I haven't had a chance to think too much about it but I'm sure when I do I will feel the way you feel now. I love the Lord so much, all I want to do is be used by him. We as humans are not perfect but as long as we are striving to live the way he wants according to his word, that is all he asks. I know holiness is tight but it is only right."

He turned to Mrs. Abney and just looked at her. He noticed the strength of a woman he has known since childhood. Only it appears that her strength in God has deepened so much that there is a peaceful countenance about her.

"Mrs. Abney, I would like to talk to you about something."

"What is it James?"

"Can we go out into the hall?"

She looked at him curiously. Without questioning she arose and they went out into the hallway.

"Mrs. Abney, there are a bunch of reporters and a crowd has swelled outside. They want answers and are waiting to talk to the doctors who worked on Rachel. They asked me some questions but I was led to a 'no comment' statement for now."

"Oh I see. Will the doctors talk to them?"

"Yes Ma'am, but they will have to get your permission first. Also, I suggest that no one should be allowed in Rachel's room unless it is hospital staff and family. It's only for the time being though. At least until Rachel regains her strength."

"I see what you mean. That would be a good idea."

"I spoke to the head nurse and the request must come from you since you are the mother and I am just a friend."

"Ok."

With that Mrs. Abney headed toward the nurse's station and made the request. The nurses were more than happy to honor the request. Just then the doctors were coming down the hallway toward Rachel's room and met Mrs. Abney as she was going in the same direction.

"How is she doing since being in a room?" Dr. Wasserman had asked.

"She was restless for a while but she is sound asleep right now."

"Before we go in and check on her we would like to talk to you about something." Dr. Smitherithers had said.

"Ok." She said while waving James and Allana toward her.

Once they came out into the corridor Dr. Wasserman began to speak.

"Mrs. Abney, the news media has picked up this story and would like a comment from us as medical professionals. Now I know what I and my colleagues had witnessed when your daughter first arrived here in the emergency room. I know what I had witnessed just a few hours after that. I must tell you that in all of my twenty plus years in the medical field I have never seen anything like this before. I know there is a God and I know what he can do.

Today my faith has been renewed therefore I am

ready to call this nothing but a miracle. I have

all the evidence, not only visually but medically.

The reports are in writing. The test showing

what was going on before we declared her dead

and the test to the contrary after we declared her

alive. I guess what I am asking is whether you

want us to go into a lot of detail or just the

basics?"

"Dr. Wasserman, I appreciate you

coming and talking to me before you spoke to

the media. What I think we better do for now is

wait. I have not had a chance to talk to Rachel

for her to understand everything that has

happened to her and I want her to be able to

make the decision as to what to tell the media.

What you can tell them is that as soon as Rachel

is able to make a decision we will let them know. Tell them it is true that she was declared dead and at what time, and tell them that she was declared alive and at what time. Details will follow."

She looked at James and Allana and they both nodded their heads in agreement. With that she turned and went back into the room. The doctors followed her so they could look Rachel over. The doctors gathered around the bed and they each checked out her arms and noticed that the bones were where they were suppose to be as well as her legs. They listened to her heart and it was pumping at a more than normal rate. Listening to her belly gave off sounds of normal bowel sounds. The doctors were hesitant about checking her eyes but did anyway. Her pupils were normal and Rachel did not stir one time while the examination was going on.

"Well, so far everything appears to be ok. We will run a battery of test later today and make a final assessment then. We will go downstairs and give a preliminary statement to the media and we will see you later after the test have been run." Dr. Wasserman said.

"Thank you so much Dr." Mrs. Abney said.

"It is my pleasure Mrs. Abney. If you have any questions or concerns, please do not hesitate to let me know. The nurses know how to get a hold of me." He stuck out his hand and shook hers and then reached for and shook James and Allana's hand as well.

The Dr.'s left the room and was talking among them selves when they were approached by a suspicious looking gentleman.

"Are you the doctors that worked on the miracle lady?"

"May I ask who is asking?"

"My name is Ronald Macy from the ATL Gazette."

"First of all, visiting hours are over. Secondly, you need to be downstairs with the other media sources. Thirdly, I will not, nor any of this staff will be answering any questions. Now either you leave or I will call security. If I find out you have come back up here or have been harassing any hospital staff I will see to it that you are barred from this hospital. Now sir, please leave."

"I'm just trying to do my job."

"I'm doing mine and that is to protect my patients. Now leave."

The reporter turned and left. Once the doctor saw that he was on the elevator and making his way down, he turned to the men and women at the nurse's station.

"If I hear of anybody giving interviews or talking to the media I will see to it that you are suspended without pay. Is that clear?" Everyone looked at him, knowing he was serious, and in unison said,

"Yes sir."

The doctors went downstairs and gave a short report to the media. They said exactly what Mrs. Abney had asked and took no questions. The media was not happy because they had deadlines to make for their particular papers and on air reports. There was nothing they could do so they went with what they had for the morning news.

Allana had decided to go to her hotel to freshen up but forgot that she had ridden in with James.

"James, I need to freshen up and I rode with you. Can you take me to the rental car?"

"I have no problem with that. Let me check with Mrs. Abney then we will be on our way."

Mrs. Abney had finally drifted to sleep and he really did not want to wake her because it had been a long and stressful day on yesterday. He went to the nurse's station and retrieved a pen and piece of paper. He not only wrote her a note and left it so she could see it but also informed the nurse who was in charge of Rachel of what he was doing?

"I should be back in about an hour or so. Please inform Mrs. Abney that if she needs me I left my cell number on the paper in room."

"Ms. Abney is in good hands. You go do what you need and get back when you can."

"Thank you."

James went to the waiting area where Allana was sitting and they headed toward the elevators.

"Everything is fine. She has both numbers and we will be back as soon as possible."

"That's fine." Allana said.

"While we are out, I might as well freshen up myself. Since I'm staying in the building where Rachel is living I think I will inform the management in case reporters try to gain access."

"Oh, that would be good. No sense in not being able to come and go with reporters sniffing around. It is not bad news but Rachel needs privacy right now."

"Right. When she is ready to tell the story she will. I had to move the car to get back in here. You want to walk with me or I can pick you up at the entrance I came back through. It's up to you."

"I'll walk. I can use the exercise." She said giggling just a little.

With that they peeked around the corner to make sure they were not seen and took off quickly to exit the hospital. They walked swiftly to the next block and got in the car and then eased into the ongoing traffic. Yesterday seemed like a distant memory and he didn't realize how tired he was behind the wheel of the car. As they were driving he decided to turn on the radio to listen to some music. The gospel station it was set on was playing an old song by the late Thomas Whitfield, Hallelujah Anyhow That song was just how it played out on yesterday. In spite of what they saw with their natural eyes it did not matter because God was up to something. The full scope of what this means has not been made clear to any of us but, God is showing himself to all who are willing to believe and receive.

Rachel was looking out of the window and realized that she was exhausted. She was thanking God within herself for helping her get to a place in him that she is able to obey his voice. If it not for him she would not be here in Atlanta on business. Everything is orchestrated by God. What she does know is that what the devil meant for bad God turned it out for the good. Her thoughts were interrupted by the news bulletin, "Woman pronounced dead, was declared alive, two hours later. It appears that we have a modern day miracle in the midst. Rachel Abney, who was in an accident on yesterday was taken to Grace and Mercy Hospital with injuries so severe that it was amazing that she was still alive. Upon receiving the best possible care she died. The doctors pronounced her dead at ten fifteen yesterday evening. By twelve fifteen she was declared alive and revived. No other explanation has been given. Her doctors and mother will give a full detailed statement at a later time."

The announcer then said, "I don't know about you brothers and sisters but I know a God that can and will do anything but fail. We will

keep you informed as we receive the
information. Pray for the family and for a
speedy recovery for Ms. Abney. All I know is
that we must be
ready at all times to meet the Lord for we know
not the day nor the hour when our ticket will be
punched to go to our eternal rest. Now Atlanta
let's hear from the man of praise, Fred
Hammond with "No Weapon."

As the music began to play, James and Rachel
exchanged glances. Then James said,

> "Listen, why don't I take you to get the
> rental car? Since your place is on the
> way back to the hospital, I'll just pick
> you up on my way back to the hospital?"

> "Are you sure? I don't want to put you

out."

"What are you talking about? I have to pass your hotel to get to the hospital anyway. It's not a problem."

"Well ok. Just call me when you are on your way."

"I'll do that. I'm going to shower, get a bite to eat then I'll come to get you."

Just then he pulled up to the church. Allana got out and got into the car. He waited to make sure the car started ok. Once she pulled off he followed her off the parking lot and they went their separate ways. Fifteen minutes later James pulled up in front of the building where he was staying and the doorman motioned for the valet to come and park the car. He went to the office and spoke to the manager, Mr. Lyle. Once James gave the information to Mr. Lyle, they shook hands.

"Mr. Rivers I will be more than happy to alert the staff to the matter at hand. Ms. Abney has only been here a short while but she is a pleasant person. Give her and her family my regards and we will make sure her mail is stopped until she returns."

"Thank you Mr. Lyle, I and her family will greatly appreciate this. I will keep you informed of her condition and estimated time of arrival back home. I believe her mother will be staying with her when she comes home."

"That will not be a problem. Is there anything we can do for you while you are here?"

"Right now I am just going to freshen up and get a bite to eat. I'll be leaving and going back to the hospital."

"If there is anything we can do for you or Ms. Abney please let us know."

"I'll do just that."

And with that James left his office and headed toward the elevators. When the doors opened he stepped on and rode to the sixth floor. His movement had slowed down just a bit because he was tired. The friend's place he was staying at had left on a trip to minister in Texas so he had the place to himself. He went to the kitchen and grabbed a glass of orange juice just to hold him until he got out of the shower. He headed toward the bedroom he was sleeping in and sat on the bed. He downed the rest of the juice and placed the glass on the night stand and lay back on the bed.

It felt so good that he started to put his feet up but decided not to do that because if he did, sleep would surely overtake him and getting up would not be easy. Instead he pulled himself up and went to the bathroom and turned on the shower. Once he stripped down and got in he adjusted the hot water to as hot as he could stand it and just stood there and let the water cascade down his tired shoulders and back. As he began to reflect over the events of the last twelve or so hours a low rumbling began to form in his belly, then he just let go and hollered, HALLELUJAH LORD. THANK YA, THANK YA, THANK YA. James began to have a praise service right there in the shower.

Allana went into her hotel room and sat down in the closest chair she could find. She knew she was tired but didn't know how much so until she sat down. She put her things down and just bowed her head. Allana started clapping her hands and thanking God for what he has done and going to do. She shouted, HALLELUJAH LORD. PRAISE YOUR HOLY NAME. As she said hallelujah, she began to feel the presence of the Lord. Allana could not sit still and got up and started dancing around the hotel room. This went on for a while. Once she composed herself, she went about getting herself refreshed by taking a shower and calling for room service. While waiting for her food she called her husband to check in and fill him in on what has happened.

"Baby, are you ok?"

"Sure, I'm fine. How are you and Davione'?"

At the hospital Mrs. Abney was awakened by transportation coming to take Rachel for her tests. She stirred slightly but was still sleeping. That was okay because she has been through a lot. Once they had taken her from the room Mrs. Abney decided to get up and get refreshed. The CNA knocked on the door and offered her services.

"Is there anything I can do for you?"

"Can I get some coffee and something to eat?"

"Sure. I'll get you a menu and you can choose for both you and your daughter. I will check her chart to see if there are any dietary restrictions."

"Thank you so much."

"I'll be right back."

Mrs. Abney proceeded to freshen up and then she called her husband, Robert.

"Hey sweetheart, I just called to tell you that Rachel is going to be just fine."

"I was just thinking about you. That's good. How are you holding up?"

"I'm doing ok. You know there is nothing like faith in God and the power of prayer. There is so much that I have to tell you. When are you coming to town?"

"I'll be there first thing tomorrow morning. My flight will be in around nine."

"Well, I will tell you everything when you get here. Just know that our baby is going to be fine. She will be glad to see you."

"Are you sure? The last we spoke it was not very pleasant."

"Trust me. God has not only healed the body but he has healed the heart. Have you talked to Kyla or Robert Jr.?"

"I told them everything I knew. They said that they would call you sometime today."

"Robert, I am going to have to stay out here with Rachel until I feel that she is capable of taking care of herself. Will that be alright with you?"

"Listen, whatever you need to do to help in her recovery is fine with me. I know how to cook."

The last statement was said with a giggle.

"Well, she is going to be having a series of test and once the doctors are satisfied with the results they will release her from the hospital."

"Ok. I'm going to have to run. I need to get to the post office and run some more errands before I leave. I love you and I'll see you in the morning."

"I love you too, honey. Do you want me to tell Rachel anything for you?"

"No. I'll tell her myself when I get there. Talk to you later."

"Alright love. See you soon."

After the final good bye they both hung up the phone. It is amazing, Mrs. Abney thought, how after forty five years of marriage how much in love the two of them were. Now that's God. Oh, we have had our share of ups and downs but we refused to throw in the towel and give up on what God had put together. James and Allana came walking into the room and interrupted her thought process.

"Glad you two made it back. You both look refreshed."

"Yes Ma'am. Since Rachel was out of danger we figured it would be ok. You were asleep and we did not want to disturb you."

Allana said.

"That's okay. I didn't realize how tired I was. I just spoke to Robert and he said his plane will be arriving around nine."

"I'll be more than happy to pick him up at the airport if you want."

"Thank you. They took Rachel to get some tests done about an hour ago. Have you two eaten? The menu is here and I was just going to order some food for myself and Rachel since she has no restrictions."

They both said in unison,

"No Ma'am."

Once the menu was sent everybody made themselves comfortable and relaxed. Since Rachel was out of the room James turned on the television searching for the news while

Allana took out her seek a word puzzle book.
Mrs. Abney just took a chair and decided to call
her daughter Kyla. The food came in and she
ate while talking to her daughter. Two hours
went by before Rachel came back to the room.
She looked tired but the color was coming back
to her. When the orderlies were done getting
her into bed and making her comfortable she
looked around at her loved ones that were there.
She took the time to look each one in their eyes.
When she got to her mother tears began to well
up. In a faint whisper she said, "I love each one
of you. Thank you for being here with me in
spite of what may have transpired before all of
this happened."

"We love you too." Her mother said.
Allana spoke up and asked,

"How are you feeling?"

"I'm tired and a little sore but other than that I'm ok. Will someone please tell me what happened? How did I end up here?"

"Are you sure you are ready? It is rather devastating." James said.

"I'm sure. Besides, I have something to tell you too."

"Well, if you are sure, he we go." James began.

For the next couple of hours James, with help from Allana, recounted what had happened including him sneaking in an area where he was not suppose to be. Rachel had some questions. She realized that her memory was a little shaky, but otherwise ok. As the events began to unfold in the story, Rachel was not afraid of what could have happened to her. The very opposite was taking hold. She had an unusual feeling of peace. Rachel did however remember her vision of being in the presence of the Lord. This she wanted to tell her family and friends but she felt it was not time yet. As James was finishing the events of the last twenty four hours the doctors came into the room.

"Rachel, how are you feeling?" Dr. Wasserman asked.

"I'm just tired and a little weak."

"With what you have been through that is to be expected. We have gone over the first few tests that have come back."

"So doc, what's the verdict?" Rachel asked smiling slightly.

"Thus far the tests for your kidneys, spleen, liver, and lungs have come back healthy and clear. No apparent damage. We are still waiting for the test examining your brain and the vessels that were damaged in the accident to come back."

"That sounds good. So when can I go home? More importantly, when can I go back to work?"

"We have to see. If everything goes well with the CT scan and MRI we may consider releasing you in a couple of days. As far as work is concerned, we'll see."

"Ok."

"Doctor," Mrs. Abney began "will she have to go through any type of rehab?"

"That was the next thing I wanted to check out. We need to see about the function of her legs and arms. Because of the breakage and then put back together we want to make sure things are ok."

"How soon will you know?"

"I am going to assign a physical therapist today and they will be here later this afternoon."

"Thank you so much for all you have done." Mrs. Abney said.

The doctors turned and began to walk away and then turned back like he forgot something.

"By the way, the media is still milling around downstairs waiting on a statement from the family. Rachel, are you up to it?"

"Up for what? What's going on?"

"Rachel, because of the nature of the accident there was widespread news. Once you were pronounced dead then alive again in a couple of hours, the news media has been camping out here at the hospital waiting for a detailed report either from me or the doctors.

Yesterday we just gave basic information." Her mother explained.

"Well, isn't that enough?" Allana answered with a chuckle,

"You know how the media is. They hear about a potential story they are on it like a dog trying to get that last piece of gristle from the bone. They won't let it go."

"I don't know what they want me to say."

"You don't have to decide right now. I will just tell them that you are in for a speedy recovery and the family will give a statement later. How is that?" Dr. Wasserman said. Mrs. Abney was looking at Rachel and said,

"No matter what you decide to do we are behind you. If you want the doctor to speak for the family, that will be fine. If you want me,

James or Allana to speak for you that will be ok with me."

"I appreciate it, but I will speak for myself. Just tell them I will make a statement tomorrow afternoon. Is that ok doctor?"

"That will be just fine Rachel. I will let them know. Now you get some rest and I will see you as soon as the other tests come back. Remember that a physical therapist will be by soon."

"Thank you."

With that the doctor and his colleagues left the room to see about their other patients. Allana, James and Mrs. Abney gathered around the bed in their chairs and got comfortable. Rachel relaxed and was soon sleeping again. While she was sleeping she began to dream about all the things that were told to her by her family and friends. In the dream she was able to recall exactly what happened on the highway that Sunday. One thing she remembered so vividly were two strong men lifting her up out of the car and placing her on the ground. She noticed how when she tried to open her eyes to see what was going on that their countenance was so bright she just closed her eyes again. Through the slits of her eyes she was able to see paramedics and firefighters doing their jobs concerning her. As she relived what happened, tears began to well the brim of her eyes and then fall down her cheeks while she slept.

Meanwhile the television was on and the news reports were the same as when James and Allana were driving back to their hotel.

"And now, an update on a story that we were covering earlier. The 'Miracle Woman', as she has been dubbed, is still in the hospital but not granting any interviews at this time. Her doctors have said that she is on her way to a full recovery and that tests so far have come back positively normal. Skeptics believe this is just a hoax and there are no such things as being dead than alive again."

"We have Katy Matthews live at Grace and Mercy hospital with a live update. Katy, what's going on? Any word yet?"

"No Simon, there has been no word yet. As you said there has been no statement from the family. But what is happening is a growing sense of agitation. There are some who believe that this is just a hoax and the reason for no statement being made is due to everyone trying to get their stories straight."

"What do you mean?" Simon asked.

"For one thing, some say that if it was a "Miracle", why not tell everybody as soon as possible. Those that have been waiting for a while do not believe in miracles because nothing like that has happened to them. We are going to stay here until we see for ourselves. This is Katy Matthews reporting live at Grace and Mercy Hospital. Now back to Simon Grant in our station."

Just then Allana turned the television off and said nothing. Then Mrs. Abney spoke. "It does not matter what others think or say. I know what I was told. I also know what I saw when I thought I was saying goodbye to my daughter. Let God be exalted and every man a lie."

"Amen" Allana said.

"Amen" James said.

About that time the Physical Therapist came in and introduced herself to everyone.

"Hello. My name is Sandy. Dr. Wasserman requested that someone come and check on the progress of this patient. Is this Rachel Abney."

"Yes it is." Mrs. Abney answered. "She is asleep right now. Can this wait until later?" she continued.

"Well, later will be tomorrow and the sooner we get the evaluation done the sooner she could possibly go home." Sandy stated.

"Ok." Mrs. Abney said while making her way to Rachel's bed.

It was at that time that she noticed tears coming down Rachel's cheeks. She started rubbing her hand and calling her name in a sweet whisper to awaken her without startling her. After a few calls of Rachel's name, her eyes flickered and then opened. Rachel looked around as if she was unaware of her surroundings. Once she was familiar as to where she was she just lay there staring.

"Rachel," Mrs. Abney began, "this is Sandy the physical therapist the doctor was talking about."

"Hello Rachel. My name is Sandy and I am here to assess your body movements and range of motion. Can you sit up for me?" Rachel began to fumble and then finding the controls situated her bed so she was sitting erect, but at an angle.

"I am going to put through a series of motion and I want you to do what you can. If at any point you start hurting then let me know. Is that fair enough?"

Finally speaking,

"Yes that's fair."

"Ok let's get started."

The others decided to step out of the room while she was being tested. James looked at his watch and noticed that it was four thirty and his stomach was doing the hungry dance.

"I'm famished. Does anyone want anything to eat?" he asked.

Allana and Mrs. Abney looked at each and Mrs. Abney spoke up and said,

"I can get something from Rachel's menu. What about you Allana?"

"I am a little famished myself. I'll go to the cafeteria with you James. I don't know what I want. Maybe something will look good once we get there."

"Let's go. Mrs. Abney, are you sure we can't get you anything?"

"I'm sure. You go ahead. I can handle things from here."

"Alright, tell Rachel we'll be right back."

"Take your time. She is okay and will continue to be ok."

When they left to go get something to eat, Mrs. Abney headed back to Rachel's room. She stood outside of the door and just watched in amazement the things she was able to do without any problems.

"You know you are the talk of the hospital." Sandy said to Rachel.

"Yeah, I've heard." Rachel replied.

"There are some who don't believe that God heals in today's time let alone raise people from the dead. One thing for sure is that he does heal and from the looks of things he raises people from the dead. Nobody can convince me otherwise."

"It has all been rather unsettling in a way. I have so many questions that I don't know where to begin."

"Well, just remember that when you have questions, the one that can give you the answers is Jesus Christ. There have been many days when I wondered why I am still at a job I thought was just a stepping stone to something else. God helped me to see that my hands are his hands touching his people. I have since resolved that I am going to be here until he tells me its time to move on. In the meantime I will just be happy to be used by him."

"So you are a Christian?"

"Yes. I know that everybody talking about heaven is not going, but I live and breathe because of the Lord. Every person I come in contact with is an opportunity for me to share my faith. God does the rest."

"I see. Don't you think you will lose your job if you are caught talking about Jesus. You know, not being political correct."

"Jesus was not politically correct when he spoke of his Father and I will not be the same."

"Something was happening to me before all of this happened. You know, in my spirit. That is why I was on my way to church. I had not been to church in years. I felt no need for God since I became an adult."

"And now how do you feel?"

"Not what I feel but what I know. God loves me and I can't live the rest of my life without him."

With that Sandy was thanking the Lord silently for another soul coming to the realization of who he is and who we are without him, nothing.

"Well Rachel, everything looks to be working just fine. Now what I want you to do is stand and take as many steps as you can. I am going to put this belt around you and I will be here every step of the way."

"I think I can do that."

After putting the belt on Rachel, Sandy helped her swing her legs to the side of the bed. She lowered the bed as far as it would go. Sandy put Rachel on a pair of hospital socks with grips on the bottoms so she would not slide across the floor.

"Are you ready?" Sandy asked her.

"As ready as I'm going to be."

"On the count of three let's do this. Remember I am here and if you feel shaky let me know and we can sit down."

"Ok."

On the third count Rachel stood up. She felt a little wobbly but otherwise ok. She took one step, then another, then another. She looked up and saw her mother standing at the door. Like a child taking her first steps she walked toward her mother with Sandy holding on to the belt. When she reached her mother she held out her arms and they embraced.

"Oh Rachel, you look good. If I didn't see it for myself nobody could have told me you were…" she trailed off and began to cry.

"Mom, I'm ok. Everything is fine. Believe me when I tell you that nothing will ever be the same again."

Just then James and Allana walked up and were floored by what they saw.

"Hey gurlie, look at you." Allana said half shrieking.

"Look out world here she comes." James chimed in.

They all embraced and then Sandy interrupted.

"Let's get the patient back into bed. We don't want to wear her out her first time out." They let go of her and watched as she made her way back to the bed. This time she was walking more steady and confident than before. When she reached her bed she sat down with a thud.

"Whew, that little bit wore me out."

"Well, you keep this up and you will be running sprints before long." Sandy chuckled. Sandy helped her get back into bed and took the belt off.

"I will give my report to the doctor and he will get with you. My prayers are with you as you make your way through your recovery and through the rest of your life."

"Thank you, Sandy. Thank you for the conversation earlier."

"Remember what I said about getting answers."

"I will."

With that Sandy made pleasantries and then left the room. The fan club came back in and was excited about what they saw. By this time it was six o'clock and dinner had arrived for Mrs. Abney and Rachel. As they prepared to eat they bowed their head and said grace. Once that was done they lifted the lid and were surprised at the great portions. They ate in silence.

"So miss Olympic sprinter, how are you feeling today?" James asked while chuckling.

"Oh, you got jokes. I'm feeling just fine. Not as tired as before but I'm ok."

"Rachel, we were so afraid for you, but God showed us that you are going to be ok." Allana said.

"Yeah. The only thing we knew we could do was pray in faith and ask God to do the rest." James added.

"Listen guys," Rachel began, "I have something to say. First I want to apologize for the things I said to each of you when we met on Saturday. I was thrown aback by my friends being born again Christians. First Allana and then James, it was too much for me to handle."

"That's ok." Allana said. Then she added "We still love you" with a huge grin on her face.

"Yeah, and we ain't going anywhere either. Forgive my bad grammar." James said laughing.

"You're forgiven. But that's not all I want to say. Allana, remember when we finished lunch and I left in a huff. Well, strange things began to start happening. For one, when I was standing at the light waiting to cross the street, when the crosswalk signaled for me to walk, a car came careening down the street as I was stepping off of the curb. I was pushed back on the curb just as the car made its way to the area where I would have been had I taken another step. Then I started hearing voices that were saying, 'I love you'. I was by myself and thought I was losing my mind. I had a dream about a man covered in blood saying nothing but reaching out his arms like he was going to grab me."

"What do you think it all means?" Allana asked.

"At first I was not sure."

"At first?" James asked.

"It was about the dream I had that made me decide to go to church. I dreamt that I was standing before God. He was calling everyone's name and either banishing them to the lake of fire or allowing them to reign with him forever."

"Where were you?" Allana asked

"Let's just say I was not a happy camper. Before he could tell me where I would spend eternity I woke up in a cold sweat. I figured it was the alcohol. You know that song Jaime Foxx has out, 'Blame it on the Alcohol', that is what I attributed the dream to."

"So that is why you decided to come to church?"

"No. That morning when you called me and were talking, you were talking but all I heard was, 'I love you'. That's when I had made up my mind, while you were talking to me."

"So what are you going to do now?" her mother asked.

"Well, I'm going to get better and play it by ear."

But Rachel knew exactly what her next plans were. It was getting late and James and Allana decided to go back to their hotels while Mrs. Abney was preparing the bed next to Rachel.

"We're going to get out of here and let you get some rest. We'll be back tomorrow morning. Mrs. Abney, we'll pick up that package on our way in so you don't have to worry about it."

"I almost forgot. Thanks James."

"What package are you talking about?" Rachel asked.

"None of your bees wax." James said smiling broadly.

"Whatever."

"Good night Rachel." He said as he kissed her on the forehead.

"Goodnight my forever friend." Allana said while giving Rachel a hug.

"It's like that now? You're not going to tell me?"

"No."

"I didn't want to know anyway, so there." She said laughing.

They both hugged Mrs. Abney and then left. Because of the press they had to use their secret exit to get out.

The next day James and Allana went to airport to pick up Rachel's dad. His flight was a few minutes late so they had to park the car and wait. Once James saw the plane land and the people started getting off of the plane he left to go get the car and waited for Allana and Mr. Abney in the lane by the baggage claim area.

Ten minutes later they were coming out and James got out so he could help with his luggage.

"James, it is good to see you again." Mr. Abney said while extending his hand to shake James'.

"It's good to see you too sir." Reaching his hand out and shaking it. "Here, let me get that." James added while putting the luggage in the trunk of the car.

Once everyone was buckled in James merged into the traffic leaving the airport and settled in for the drive.

"Allana was filling me in on what happened. It is incredible what God will do for you. How is Rachel doing?"

"She was ok when we saw her last night. I'm sure she is ok." James said.

"I called your wife when I saw your plane land. She said Rachel had a peaceful rest and had a good breakfast. She was in physical therapy and due back at any time."

"That's great. I know she will be surprised to see me, but will she be happy to see me?" Mr. Abney questioned.

"Mr. Abney, she's a changed person. She will definitely be glad to see you." James said with confidence.

Everyone got caught up in what had been going on in their lives while they were riding to the hospital. When they pulled up to the hospital the crowd was still hanging out, and the media that started out being two maybe three stations has swelled to over ten stations and their affiliates. James had to do some maneuvering in order to get through without being noticed. He headed toward his private spot and parked the car.

Once they were inside the hospital they made their way to the sixth floor and started walking toward Rachel's room. As they rounded the corner of her corridor the physical therapist and Rachel were walking out of the room with Sandy the therapist holding onto her belt. Mr. Abney called out Rachel's name. When Rachel heard her name she looked up and a beam of light shone on her face. Although Mr. Abney was up in age he was still spry and made quick steps toward his daughter. With Sandy in tow Rachel moved quickly toward her father. When they reached each other they embraced each other. They separated and just stared at each other for what seemed like forever.

"Daddy, when did you get here?"

"About an hour ago, James and Allana picked me up at the airport."

Rachel looked at James and Allana and then smiled.

"This is what you two were up to." Rachel said.

"Daddy, I am so glad to see you. You look good."

"Me? You're the one who was in an accident. They filled me in as to the goings on around here. I'm just thankful you are alright."

"I am too. How long are you going to stay?"

"I will stay as long as you want me too." When they reached her room he eyed his wife and gave her a hug and a kiss.

"How are you sweetie?" he asked.

"I'm just fine. I'm glad you're here though. Have you eaten?"

"Not yet. I was too anxious and my stomach was in knots. Now that I see my two favorite girls I'll eat in a little bit."

As they all settled in Rachel's room Sandy gave them some information.

"Rachel, your walking has improved to such that if when I come back this afternoon and you can walk ten feet steady without the belt I am going to suggest that you be released."

"Are you serious?"

"Yes. Your progress has been phenomenal. There is no reason, unless the doctors see a problem, why you should stay for any longer than necessary."

"Thank you Sandy."

"No, thank you. It is good for me when I am able to see the results of God work. I will be back this afternoon and we will go from there. Enjoy your family and I'll see you later."

"Ok. Thanks."

Sandy left the room and a sigh of relief was made by all. Allana excused herself from the room.

"I'm going to step into the hallway and call my husband and give him an update."

"Tell him I said hello for me." Rachel said.

"I will do just that."

Allana left the room and made the call to her husband. As she walked and talked she decided to go to the gift shop. Once she got there she bought her friend a get well Mylar balloon, some flowers and a card.

"Listen baby, I'll call you later. I just wanted to give you an update of what was going on. If you don't mind I would like to stay until Rachel is released from the hospital."

"That's fine. I miss you though." Her husband Savione' said.

"I know, and I miss you too. I love you and will be home real soon."

"When do they expect her to be released?"

"Prayerfully, in the next couple of days."

"Well, call me tonight before you go to bed. Tell Rachel I'm praying for her and give her my love."

"I will. Savione', I just want to say thank you."

"For what?"

"For you being a good husband and very understanding. I love you and I will call you later."

With goodies in hand, Allana made her way back to her friend's room but ran into a problem. While talking on the phone, unbeknownst to her, a reporter was listening and followed her out of the gift shop and started asking questions. She was shocked and decided that leading him back to the room was not a good idea. Allana ducked into a restroom and stayed about ten minutes. When she opened the door he was standing right there waiting on her. She decided to make a phone call.

"I can't get back to the room because there is a reporter harassing me. Will you come and get me?"

"I'll be right there. Where are you?"

"I'm sitting in front of the gift shop.

Hurry, he has called for reinforcements."

"Don't move. I'm on my way."

Allana hung up the phone and started getting

nervous. The reporter was asking her a lot of

questions and would not leave her alone.

Finally James came around the corner and spoke

to the reporter.

"Listen jack."

"The name is Terry. Terry Jones. I just

want to ask a few questions."

"Did you not get the memo? We are not

granting interviews and when we do we will let

you know."

"I'm just trying to do my job. Just

answer a few questions, please?"

"The answer is no. Now get lost. If you follow us I will call the police and charge you with harassment."

Terry Jones put his pencil and paper back into his inside jacket pocket and turned to walk away. James motioned for Allana to get up and start walking. To make sure that they were not followed they went in the opposite direction of where they should have gone. Once they felt it was safe they took the elevator up three floors, got off and headed for the stairwell and took the stairs. This went on for a couple days. The ducking and dodging was getting old. Finally the day came, Thursday, when Rachel was given the great news of being released to go home.

"Rachel, we have to make a decision." Dr. Wasserman said.

"What decision is that?"

"You have to decide when you are going to hold a press conference. You have been labeled "The Miracle Lady" and the people want some answers."

"I know what I have to do. Would you please set it up for me Dr. Wasserman?"

"I will be more than happy to. I can give them the medical aspect of what happened and you can answer the questions. We will set it up for your release day which will be tomorrow morning. I will make sure that it takes no longer than a half hour then you can go home from there. Is that alright with you and your family?"

Rachel looked around at everybody and they all gave a nod of approval.

"Yes, Dr. Wasserman that will be fine."

"Before I go I just want to say how much of a pleasure it has been being your physician during this trying but happy time. As I explained to your mother, I had faith but through a series of issues in my life it had been shaken and I was at a crossroads of doubt and unbelief. God bringing you back to life has given me great resolve to know that no matter what I go through, he is with me and has given me strength go forward. Since that night I have recommitted my life back to serving him." With tears welling up he continued,

"This is not about a study of medicine but about what God can and will do if we just take him out of the box. I understand that when we truly trust him, no matter our profession, it's not just another day. "

"Dr. Wasserman, you are a testament that when miracles happen you are not so pious in your book learning to acknowledge God as the ultimate healer." Rachel's father stated.

Though they both reached for the others hand to shake, they ended up in a warm embrace. The doctor broke down and cried on Mr. Abney's shoulder. He forgot about decorum and medical protocol. He forgot about what was inappropriate. Dr. Wasserman knew that he was in the presence of God with the believers in the room. After about a minute he pulled away and headed out of the room, but not before grabbing some tissue from the bathroom and wiping his face.

"Well is such a deep subject I'll just stick to the shallow end of the pool."

"What are you talking about Robert?"
Mrs. Abney asked.

"Only God can mend the hearts of broken men. I would have never expected that to happen."

"But what does that have to do with a well?" She chuckled.

Then everyone began to laugh. They laughed so hard that the nurses came in and wanted to know if everything was ok.

"Everything is fine. You had to be here."

When the nurses left the room they broke out into laughter again. They finally settled down long enough for Rachel to ask James a question.

"James, will you do something for me?"

"Sure, what do you need?"

"When we have the press conference, will you answer the questions for me? I will talk too but I need you to set the tone of the press conference."

"I can do that. Is there anything else?"

"I think that will do it. Mom and Dad will both stay with me at my place?"

"That was a given." Her mother said.

"Allana, when are you going back home?"

"I have my laptop so I can work and do my schooling from anywhere. Savione' told me to take my time and he sends his love and prayers. I also told him that as soon as you are released and all is well, then I will come home."

"Good. I won't keep you from your hubby too much longer." She said with a pouty kissy face.

The next couple of days went by without incidence. It was finally time for Rachel to be discharged from the hospital. Allana drove her rental car so there would be enough room for everyone. The nurses let them borrow a cart to haul all of the flower planters, balloons and get well cards that she had received. In order to be able to leave without being followed, the plan was to carry everything to the car that had been parked in the back by the loading docks. This was compliments of Dr. Wasserman. After the press conference they are to get on the elevator like she was going back to her room. Once the coast is clear they would leave by the service elevator.

A podium and some chairs had been set up for the family. The crowd was frenzied and hurried because they were trying to get their equipment set up for a live feed for the various news stations that had arrived. When Dr. Wasserman had stood at the podium a hush spread quickly throughout the area.

"My name is Dr. Wasserman I am here to give you the information that you have been waiting on. It would be greatly appreciated if you would hold all questions until the end of both speeches. Ms. Rachel Abney was brought into Grace and Mercy Hospital on Sunday morning with severe injuries. She was rushed into the operating room where it was assessed that it was dire to stop the bleeding in her brain and to the repair the puncture in her lungs. Once we were able to medically get her stable we closed her wounds with the anticipation of further surgery to correct the least critical injuries at a later time".

"Ms. Abney appeared to be stable and then she flat lined, meaning that all of her vital organs, heart and blood pressure had stopped. We did all we could do to revive her but to no avail. She was pronounced dead at ten fifteen pm Sunday night. We waited for her mother, who was on her way, before sending her to the morgue. While saying goodbye some things transpired while her friend was in the room alone. I will now give the microphone over to her friend James."

"Thank you Dr. Wasserman. My name is James Rivers. I am Rachel's childhood friend. As Dr. Wasserman stated, I had asked them to leave the room because I wanted to say my own personal good byes. You see, we were sweethearts back in the day and I wanted to let her know that I would always love her. Before I could say what I wanted, I was overcome with grief. You see, I am a Bible believing Christian. I believe that God saves souls, that he heals the sick, raises the dead and is a deliverer. While I was praying, I was told by God what to do and I did it. Rachel is sitting here now not because of anything I had done but because of what God has done. He raised her from that death bed and she was declared alive again at twelve fifteen, two hours after she was pronounced dead.

As you can see for yourself, everything that the doctor has said is true. Except for a little weakness in her legs, she is totally healed. Though God has healed her physical body, he will also heal the spiritual body which is the most important. The bible says 'God so loved the world that he gave his only begotten Son, that whosoever believes in Him should not perish but shall have everlasting life." John 3:16. There is a reason for Rachel being raised from the dead and that reason will be shown to her in due time. That is all I have for you. Thank you."

Then the barrage of questions began.

"This is Jeffrey Steele of Channel 8 News. How do know that she was as bad off as the report says?"

"What you will need to do is talk to the paramedics and firefighters who put the flames out on her car" James answered,

"My name is Kelly Bryant with WATL and I would like to ask Ms. Abney a question. Do you remember what happened and how do you feel right now?"

Rachel took her time. She wanted to tell everything but knew the time was not right.

What she did say brought it straight to the point. Rachel stood at the microphone and held on to the sides while James stood close. A hush fell over the throng of people that had invaded the area.

"To Ms. Bryant and the rest of the media, make no mistake. God is to be given praise today for allowing me to be standing here. Yes I was once dead but now I am alive. God is good and merciful. The facts remain. At a later date my medical record will be available online so you can see for yourself what God has healed me from. Not only did he heal my physical body but my spiritual body. He has rescued me from spending eternity in hell. That is all I have to say."

By the time Rachel had finished her speech, the press conference was over. There was a barge of questions as Rachel and her family and friends made their way to the elevator. When they were out of sight, the media scrambled to phones and using their cell phones to text to their various stations what was said. Once they reached the sixth floor they sat in the lobby until they were given the ok to leave.

"Allana, were you serious about putting the information online?" Her dad asked.

"Yes dad, but when it is time."

They were given the word that it was clear for them to leave. James would take Rachel in his car and Allana would take the Abney's in her car. When Rachel got in the car she asked James a question.

"That church I was going to on last Sunday, are they open right now?"

"I don't know, why?"

"Can you call them before we take off? There is something I need to do."

"Sure."

James looked through his phone directory and then called.

"Yes, how much longer are you going to be there?" Oh, ok. Thank you."

"They are open because they are having a meeting and service tonight."

"I need to go there before we get to my place."

"We need to get you home."

"James, this is something that cannot wait. Will you please take me to the church?"

"If you are sure I'll take you?"

"I'm sure."

"What about them?" as he pointed to the car behind him.

"They can come too. I wouldn't have it any other way."

James started the car and headed toward the church. When they came to the area of the accident, Rachel tensed a little then breathed, "Thank you Lord." When they arrived at the church James got out and so did Allana.

"What are we doing her?" Allana asked.

"She wanted to come here. She said it was something she had to do. Go get her parents and come on in."

When they got into the church, they were greeted by the assistant minister who was very nice. He recognized Rachel from the news reports.

"Welcome. I am glad to see the wonderful works of God. What can we do for you here at The One Way to Christ Church Apostolic Church where the honorable Bishop Tyson Finnell is pastor?"

"I want to be baptized." Rachel stated. Everybody looked at each and gasped.

"Rachel what's going on?" her mother asked.

"Rachel, are you sure this is the right time? You just got out of the hospital." Allana asked.

Rachel looked at each one of them and said,

"As we have seen in the last week that tomorrow is not promised. I have kept God at bay all of my adult life. He has done nothing for me but good and he has been faithful in watching over me even when I was not faithful in acknowledging him. It's time. I may not live to see Sunday, therefore I need to get things right today."

"Oh Rachel, I am so happy for you and proud of you. My prayers have been answered for these twenty some years." Her mother said while choking back tears.

"Praise the Lord. I can baptize you right now." The assistant Pastor said.

"Excuse me. I'm sorry, what is your name?"

"My name is Garry V. Jackson."

"If it is ok, I would like to be baptized by my friend, Minister James Rivers."

"It is rather unusual but that can be arranged. Follow me."

Everyone followed Minister Jackson to an area of the church that turned out to be the dressing rooms for those being baptized.

"You can change in here." He told the Rachel as he pointed to the room.

"Sir, you can change over here. Let me know when you are ready."

Allana and Mrs. Abney helped Rachel get dressed while James got dressed. Once everyone was ready they met at the baptismal pool behind the choir stand on the pulpit. James was already in the water praying. When Rachel came into view, she was strong enough to hold onto the rails and walk down into the water with the assistance of James when she reached the bottom step. They moved toward the other end so there would be room when he immersed her in the water.

"Are you ready?" James answered as he was holding her steady.

"I am long overdue. Yes I'm more than ready."

"Here we go."
With her parents and best girlfriend looking on he proceeded.

"Rachel by the confession of your faith in the death, burial and resurrection of the Lord Jesus Christ, I now baptize you in the name of Jesus for the remission of your sins and you shall receive the gift of the Holy Ghost."

With that he immersed Rachel all the way under and brought her back up. When she came up she was praising God and speaking in her heavenly language. Everyone had begun to praise God because the meeting had been put on hold until the soul had gone down in Jesus

Name.

ONE YEAR LATER......

James and Rachel have renewed their

love for one another. Rachel is still receiving

requests from television and radio to do

interviews of what happened to her. Her walk

with God gets stronger everyday. God has

given her the gift of healing so she and James

minister together. He preaches and with the

Holy Spirit's leading she lay hands on the sick

and prays. Some are healed right away, while

others send reports of complete healing later on

down the line. They are engaged to be married.

Rachel still works for the investment

company. She works full time there and travels

on the weekends.

Allana received her Master's in Business and opened her own Accounting business that she runs with her husband Savione'.

Mr. and Mrs. Abney are still madly in love. They have become quite popular because of their daughter. They now travel more and ministers to people about the strength of God and about never giving up on their loved ones by praying and believing that God will do what he says he will do.

Dr. Wasserman and his colleagues Dr. Smitherrithers and Dr. Stein still work for Grace and Mercy Hospital, but run a free clinic in poorest area of Atlanta.

"It is of the Lords mercy that we are not consumed, because his compassions fail not, they are new every morning, great is thy faithfulness." Lamentations 3:22

Not the end but a brand new beginning.

Acknowledgements

First and foremost I would like to thank my Lord, Jesus Christ. It is a fact that without him I would not be.

I would like to thank my Mother, Patricia Walls, for her unconditional love and support and many prayers for me in all of my adventurous endeavors. Mom, I thank God for giving you to me as a mother. I love you very much.

Thank you to my sister, Lisa Walls, who took up the mantle of making sure that I understand what being a loving sibling is about. Words will never be enough to express just how much I appreciate you.

To my cousin Jennifer Young-Tait, who has gone on to be with the Lord, thank you for being the inspiration and encouragement behind this project. For the rest of my life I will be one of the many telling your son Solomon about the ray of sunshine of a mother he would have been proud to know.

To ALL of my friends old and new, and too many to name for fear of leaving someone out, THANK YOU!!! Your love and patience with me as I talked incessantly about this book is duly noted. LOL! Thank you for your prayers and love. Each of you has a special place in my heart and I love you all.

GOD DID IT!!!